THE MYSTERY OF CROAKER'S ISLAND

× × ×

LINDA DeMEULEMEESTER

WANDERING FOX

An imprint of
HERITAGE HOUSE PUBLISHING
Victoria | Vancouver | Calgary

Wandering Fox Books
An imprint of
Heritage House Publishing Company Ltd.
heritagehouse.ca

*Cataloguing information available from
Library and Archives Canada*

978-1-77203-251-2 (pbk)
978-1-77203-252-9 (epub)

Edited by Lesley Cameron
Cover and interior design by Setareh Ashrafologhalai
Cover illustration by Alyssa Koski

The interior of this book was produced on 100% post-consumer recycled paper, processed chlorine free, and printed with vegetable-based inks.

We acknowledge the financial support of the Government of Canada through the Canada Book Fund (CBF) and the Canada Council for the Arts, and the Province of British Columbia through the British Columbia Arts Council and the Book Publishing Tax Credit.

  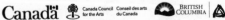

22 21 20 19 18 1 2 3 4 5

Printed in Canada

To John, Alec,
and Joey with love

× 1 ×

A QUESTIONABLE QUEST

SAM NOVAK FROZE on the spot when the tiny pot-bellied man wearing eye-glasses as thick as pop bottles and carrying a black leather satchel passed him on the street. After the man had scurried by, Sam turned and stared after him. Not because the man was a grown-up who was shorter than he was, or because the man's face had odd bumps, or even because enormous hairy ears poked out of the man's white mane— that would be impolite. Sam stared because when the man had passed him, the hair on the nape of Sam's neck bristled. A chill crept over him as if an Arctic wind had suddenly channelled through Hecate Strait, cut along the coastline, and blasted Sam head-on.

The man continued to scuttle down the street, kicking up brittle yellow and red leaves that tossed around like a kaleidoscope. Sam blinked twice, shouldered his heavy backpack, and then cut through the high school parking lot. He ran straight into Dory, which was the last thing he wanted.

Dory was holding court with a group of trendy-looking worshippers who'd fallen under her thrall. Dory had the kind of appearance and confidence that let her soar to the top. If anyone bothered to take a closer look, which in Sam's experience nobody did, they would notice the sinister twist in her smile and the diabolical arch of her eyebrows.

"I distinctly said I'd give you a ride home in *an hour*." Dory narrowed her green eyes and wound a strand of blond-streaked hair around her finger. "You're not expecting to hang around here with *me*, are you?" She didn't even try to hide the disbelief in her voice.

Sam's face burned. "No, I have ... stuff ... to do."

Then, with not so much as a backward glance, she dismissed him. As Sam walked away, he knew he was meant to hear what followed.

"Although I find your seaside town, Croaker's Cove, quaintly charming, mates," Dory said, "I'm stuck here against my will, suddenly the older sister to a weird little twelve-year-old brother."

Little? Weird? Sam straightened his too long, too loosely knit sweater that his grandmother had made for him, and tried to slick back the wayward cowlick in his mop of brown hair. He was sure the single zit that had appeared on his chin that morning glowed like a neon light.

Dory wasn't *that* much older than Sam, only four years, once he turned thirteen in another eight weeks. And technically, he wasn't 100 percent her brother. She was his half-sister from their dad's first marriage.

Dory was the biggest obstacle holding Sam back from what he wanted—a permanent home in Croaker's Cove.

After Sam's mother died, Sam had moved to different countries every year because his father, Captain Jake Novak, travelled with his military work. Then his father would be called away again after a few months, and Sam would end up in one boarding school after another. He hated the wandering life. His father had agreed that Sam and his little sister, Molly, who was just starting school, could both stay with their grandmother on a *trial basis* for now. This was Sam's chance for a real home. He could make friends he didn't have to say goodbye to at the end of the school year. Except...

This arrangement took an unexpected turn when it suddenly included Dory, his older half-sister, a.k.a. the evil witch of the South. What was with Dory's accent? She'd only lived in Australia for a few months before coming back to Canada.

Dory's mother was remarrying and had told Sam and Dory's father that she was "in the middle of things," and had asked that Dory stay with them during Australia's winter school break. Sam's father thought Dory could live with Sam and Molly for the whole year and help their grandmother.

Dory was the *opposite* of helpful, which left Sam in what his babcia called a pickle. Sam knew, as sure as the zit throbbing on his chin, that if he didn't make this work and prove they could all get along and cause no worries to their grandmother, it would be boarding school again!

Shake it off, whispered a calm voice in his head—a voice Sam liked to think had been his mother's. He felt her presence here, as if the constant sea breeze carried her scent. Sam turned down one more street. His stomach began cartwheeling. He climbed the steps up to the huge black door of a sprawling white house and stared at the doorbell, willing his hand to press the button. He hesitated.

In video and board games, a hero got a quest and it was fun. In real life, being given a quest was nerve-wracking. Sam's school counsellor, Ms. Dickens, had given Sam *this* quest.

She'd tapped Sam on the shoulder and handed him a pile of books, saying, "Blake's mother asked if the new boy would drop these books off at his home. Blake doesn't want to see any of his regular friends yet."

Ms. Dickens had looked at Sam's frown and quickly added, "His mother says Blake remembers you from grade two and is looking forward to your visit."

Sam didn't remember Blake, and he doubted Blake had ever noticed him. This was a questionable quest at best. Once more, Sam raised his hand to press the doorbell. Then he glimpsed a flash of metal out of the corner of his eye. He turned his head in surprise.

The peculiar man he'd passed earlier was standing behind the hedge next door. Sam was sure that the man was purposely hiding behind the thicket of tall shrubs. From his leather satchel, he unwound a long coil of wire and dropped an object shaped like a curved triangle off the steep bluff. Then he took out an electronic device that wasn't a cellphone or a tablet. The device glinted silver in the sunlight.

Spotting Sam, the little man quickly dropped the device back into his satchel and disappeared into the shadows of the garden.

× 2 ×

MYSTERIES OF
THE DEEP

SAM PEERED AT the bushes, but the strange little man was nowhere to be seen. He shrugged his shoulders and reached for the doorbell.

"Hey, wait up!" a voice called from behind.

Sam turned around. His jaw dropped, but he quickly closed his mouth. Khallie Saran rushed up the brick steps and joined him. When she shot him a nervous smile, her perfect teeth gleamed white. Sam's hands started to sweat.

"Hi, Sam. I overheard Ms. Dickens asking you to come here, and I've been trying to catch up with you." Khallie took a deep breath.

Sam might have no recollection of Blake from before, but he remembered *her*. Boys had been literally chasing Khallie since preschool. He only used to watch from the sidelines as she'd turn her head over her shoulder and laugh as she outraced them all. Even though he was a fast runner, Sam never thought himself worthy of chasing the princess of Seaside Elementary.

Khallie Saran knew *his* name?

"Can I carry some of Blake's work so it looks like the counsellor sent me with you?" Khallie reached out expectantly. Like a robot, Sam opened his backpack.

"I've wanted to talk to Blake for ages, but his mother keeps saying he's not seeing visitors." Khallie rubbed the back of her neck. "Ow, I guess I've got a mosquito bite—should there be mosquitoes this late in September? I don't remember insects buzzing around this long past summer. Is it a mosquito bite?"

Khallie turned and bent her head, and her black hair tumbled forward like a curtain of silk. Sam leaned over, trying not to breathe on the back of her neck. "I don't see an insect bite, but you have three deep scratches," said Sam. The marks looked red and angry. "You should put antiseptic on those."

Khallie dropped her hair and turned back. All the while she kept chattering about Blake not returning messages, unaware it was all Sam could do to keep his mouth from gaping and catching flies, not that he'd noticed any insects.

"I miss him, you know." Khallie's bright smile slipped from her face. "We weren't going out exactly. There's no way I'd be allowed to date a boy until I'm like forty." She gave a little laugh and her smile returned. "My parents are super strict." Her laughter sounded like soft musical bells.

Khallie reached into Sam's backpack and yanked out a book. "So is it okay if it looks like I'm bringing him this? So can I come with...?"

Smile at the girl, came that soft voice. *Say something.* "Uh, sure," said Sam.

Khallie didn't hesitate when she leaned over to ring the doorbell. They could hear footsteps coming toward the door. Sam suddenly thought, *what do I say to a person in Blake's situation?* Not, *how are you feeling...* Not, *so what's new...*

The door flew open. A woman dressed like a lawyer or somebody's boss stood in front of them. *But she's a glass lady,* Sam thought, like those porcelain figures in his grandmother's china cabinet ready to shatter from a sudden noise or the slightest tap. Her eyes widened a little at the sight of Khallie, who shuffled uneasily and then held out the book as if she was presenting a hall pass.

"Hello, Mrs. Evans. I'm bringing books," Khallie said. "Like Sam here." She managed to smile, even though Mrs. Evans wrung her hands in a way that made Sam think she was more nervous than them—which didn't help how he felt about his quest. Mrs. Evans ushered them inside.

Sam gazed around. Blake's house couldn't look more different than his. There was so much space, and not a smidge of colour—everything dissolved into a haze of white curtains and walls...

The grand home even hushed Khallie's constant chatter. "Blake, you have visitors," announced Blake's mother in a not-quite-there voice. She led Sam and Khallie into the den. Blake sat on a spindle chair. He was pale under his blond hair, making Sam think of an old photograph that had faded. He almost blended into the walls and furniture that surrounded him.

"Hi. You brought the books?" Blake looked as stiff as his chair. He glanced at Khallie, and something unreadable crossed his face. "Long time no see."

"Hello, Blake." Khallie handed Blake the book, and said with what Sam thought was forced cheerfulness, "I wanted to come so I could tell you that I'm volunteering at the community centre. There's a new program—basketball for people in..."

She didn't finish the sentence. The look on Blake's face did that for her. "You're kidding, right?" he said.

For the first time, Sam noticed Khallie had dark smudges under her eyes. She rubbed the back of her neck again as she shook her head. "Sorry."

Ignoring her, Blake pointed at Sam's backpack. Sam swallowed a lump of spit that had gathered in his throat. It was his turn.

"Ah, Ms. Dickens suggested that I bring you your library books and for me to ask you if..." Instead of finishing his sentence, Sam brought out the board game he'd stuffed in his pack—Star Trek Canaan. "She . . . thought maybe you'd like to join the gaming club after school."

"I don't want to join the gaming group." Blake's face darkened. "Those guys are losers."

Playing board games meant wherever Sam moved, he could join a club and make instant friends. Sam hadn't cared what other people thought—he'd never stayed long enough in one place to worry about those things.

Maybe Blake didn't want new friends. But Ms. Dickens had said he hadn't been interested in seeing his old friends either. Sam didn't know what to say. Instead, he let his gaze wander and fasten on the shadow in the hall, lurking like an uninvited guest. He turned back and flinched under Khallie's accusatory gaze.

"Sorry." Sam swallowed. "The counsellor said . . ." Sam looked away again. "I thought . . ."

"Thought what?" Blake challenged.

"Sorry," Sam mumbled again.

Everything Sam said was making this worse. He focused on a bookshelf stacked with gold and silver sports trophies glinting in the sunlit room. When he looked away, he saw Blake was staring at him. Sam's face heated up and he began to say sorry again, but Blake held up his hand.

"For the record, there's no point in you both saying sorry over and over. Sorry doesn't help." Blake waved his hand. "Board games didn't interest me before my skiing accident, so why should they now? I haven't changed... ah." Blake rubbed his legs, and when he saw Sam and Khallie's uncomfortable expressions, it was his turn to go red. He dropped his arm. Then he sighed and gestured to the wheelchair in the hallway. "Okay, I guess I've changed a little. But this is only temporary."

Khallie's eyes glistened as she bit her lip, probably holding back another "sorry." Sam didn't know what to say. Instead, he began hauling out the books he'd brought for Blake.

Sam hadn't even looked at the stack of books the counsellor had given him for Blake. "These books are on oceans; that's my grandmother's field of study. She works at the Ocean Institute. She could give you lots of information..." Sam flipped over the last book. It would definitely *not* meet with his babcia's approval— *Unexplained Mysteries of the Deep...* Sam couldn't resist checking out the back cover.

"Don't tell *anyone* about these books." Blake glared at Sam and Khallie. "I don't want people thinking I'm geeking out. I've got a reputation to preserve." He gave a bitter laugh.

Khallie nodded. Sam shrugged his shoulders. Even though his grandmother didn't encourage what she called spooky science, he pointed to the book on ocean mysteries. "I'd like to read that one."

Blake levelled Sam with a serious gaze like he was sizing him up. Then he took a breath, reached over to the table beside him, and flipped open an expensive laptop. "I wanted some books on oceanography because I've, ah, had some time on my hands." Blake gazed fiercely at the screen. "So I've been following the underwater monitors at the Ocean Institute." Blake's face flushed as if he was confessing the most embarrassing thing ever.

"See anything interesting?" Khallie scratched her neck.

"Ah, sort of..." Blake tilted his head. "Mostly I've been checking the audio feed from hydrophones that they've sunk into the ocean trench offshore."

"Those are underwater microphones," Sam added after seeing Khallie's confused expression.

"Exactly." Blake ran his fingers through his hair. "I need someone to help me figure out where *this* signal's coming from."

Blake spun the laptop around and showed them a screen filled with weird, wiggly lines. Looking at Khallie again, he said, "Spectrograms are visual patterns of sound. The longer the wave lines, the louder the sound."

Khallie muttered, "You don't have to dumb *everything* down for me."

Sam never minded clear and detailed explanations, although because his grandmother was an oceanographer, he knew what spectrograms were.

But something was wrong with that one.

Sam shook his head and pointed at the screen. "That can't be."

Blake let out a nervous laugh. "I know. If I'm reading the signal right, it's a huge sound wave, *like from a giant sea monster.*"

× 3 ×

NERD TRAIN

GIANT MONSTERS in the ocean—that was crazy talk. But Sam didn't point that out to Blake. Instead, he studied Blake's laptop screen and the way the sound waves spiked into a series of jagged points.

"Even *I* know that over 95 percent of the oceans are unexplored," Khallie said, a touch defensively. "And off our coast, the ocean is *very* deep." She shrugged her shoulders. "Why wouldn't there be a giant squid or two?"

Sam shook his head. "I've never heard of giant squids being discovered in the northern hemisphere." He kept staring at the spectrogram on the screen. Yellow and red curves spiked against a static blue and purple background. Squids or no squids, the spikes showed the recording of a *huge* underwater noise.

"Weird, huh?" said Blake. "For all we know it could be echoes from a school of sea monsters." He laughed again.

"Or secret military weapons," mused Sam. "Have you reported this echo to the Ocean Institute yet?" He leaned over until his nose almost touched the laptop screen.

Blake shook his head. "I'm not reporting anything until I find out more about the signal. I want to make sure I'm not misreading it, so I don't end up looking like some kind of clown."

"Hmm, sea monsters and secret weapons..." Khallie smiled. "Don't you think you both know too much about weird ocean stuff to be considered normal, anyway?" She was teasing him, but from the way she looked at Blake, Sam figured Blake could say he beamed up to Mars every Saturday night and she'd believe him.

Sam got that Blake wasn't in a rush to report this. The signal couldn't be right. "There are lots of sounds in the ocean, but a sound wave this loud?"

Khallie rubbed the back of her neck again. "Who'd have thought the ocean was so noisy? I never hear much when I'm underwater."

"Whales, submarines, boats all make noise that can be identified, but this spectrogram isn't showing those noise patterns," said Blake. "These sounds are much more mysterious."

As they stared intensely at the spectrogram of the strange ocean echo, Blake's mom brought in a tray of drinks and chocolate chip cookies. After downing a soda, Sam checked his watch. He stood up, mindful not to drop any cookie crumbs on the expensive white rug. "I've got to go; my... um... sis... ter, um... Dory, is giving me a ride home."

"That's the new girl who keeps driving up and down the main street in the cherry red convertible, right?" Khallie rolled her eyes, making Sam smile.

"A 1982 Fiat Spider, to be exact," Sam added wistfully. He'd always thought he'd be the one who would get to drive their father's old sports car.

"Sweet," said Blake.

Sam nodded. "And it torques at 3600 RPM."

Blake grinned approvingly, and Khallie rolled her eyes again.

"You wouldn't want to help me figure out this sound wave, would you?" Blake asked Sam. "Do you know anybody in that game club who's familiar with sound waves and radio bands?"

"That would be Owen Chatterjee," Khallie cut in before Sam could answer. "He's been building radio sets since forever. He's always talking about signals and bands and sound waves and tons of science stuff in class."

"Chatterjee?" Blake grimaced. "Talk about jumping on the nerd train."

"Well, if you want a radio expert, suck it up," Khallie said firmly. "Why don't we meet back here tomorrow, and I'll bring Owen?"

Blake let out a reluctant sigh. "I guess."

Sam kept his mouth shut—he'd met Owen, and while the kid did seem ... odd, he was a good gamer. But Sam was beginning to get the lay of the land here. It sounded like you could only belong to one team—the cool jocks or the nerdy gamers. You definitely couldn't be different. He glanced at the wheelchair and thought how Blake kept himself hidden.

Sam looked at his watch again. "Yikes, I've really gotta go." He flew out of the house as Blake and Khallie shouted their goodbyes.

× × ×

SAM BROKE INTO a jog as he hurried to catch up with Dory. He liked running; it cleared his mind. Maybe he'd try out for the track team at school and be accepted into Blake and Khallie's group. He'd already decided he liked Khallie. He thought he *could* like Blake; they had some stuff in common.

Only, Sam also liked gaming. Besides, there was his whole problem about how he crumbled under pressure and cost the team. He'd been cut from track at his old school. It was a sore spot between him and his father.

"Get back on the horse," his father had said after Sam had been cut. Sam would happily get on a horse—he just had no interest in competing again.

Dory's car had vanished from the school parking lot, and it was a long trek back to the beach house. Sam sighed and headed for the bus stop, noticing yet another poster of a missing cat tacked onto a telephone pole. That was the third one he'd seen this week. He'd better remind his little sister, Molly, to keep a close eye on her cat, Pix.

When Sam crossed onto the main street, he spotted the red Fiat parked in front of a café, and perched on an outdoor patio chair was Dory, slurping frothy drinks with two of her friends. When she spotted Sam, a slight twinge of guilt darted across her face.

She waved him over. "It's about time you showed up. I've been waiting," she said in a totally unconvincing way. "Let's go," she said to the other girls.

Sam climbed into the back of the Fiat Spider. The tiny car only had two tiny fold-down backseats, forcing him to jam himself so close to Dory's friend Gina that the highway suddenly seemed to stretch out forever. Sam's face flushed at the older girl's nearness, and he was sure it made the zit on his chin glow like a searchlight. Her flowery perfume made his eyes water, and he held back a sneeze. Worse, during the drive, Sam had to sit and listen to the girls discuss whether vampires or werewolves would make better boyfriends.

Just when he couldn't listen one second longer to girl-talk, and he wanted to yell, "There's no such thing as vampires"—or even more desperately, "Stop the car. Let me out!"—he heard something that made his ears prick up...

The subject had switched to where vampires would most likely hang out, and Dory's friends had agreed it could only be one place—in the haunted old mansion on Croaker's Island up the coast.

"Totally," said the girl in the front seat, Angel Chan. "There've been reports of mysterious sounds and lights on that island for ages, and no one has ever stayed in the Sinistrus Mansion for more than a week. My aunt works for the real estate office, and they gave up years ago trying to sell the house or even rent it for the summer."

"Did you say the island has strange sounds?" asked Sam. He wondered if the eerie recordings Blake had picked up on the spectrogram were radio signals bouncing off sunken debris around the island. For some reason, the image of the strange little man with the silver device flashed into Sam's mind...

"So is it Sinistrus Mansion or Croaker's Island that's haunted, mates?" Dory turned her car onto the narrower coastal road and passed a rundown trailer park. "How much farther?" she asked.

"We're almost there," said Gina. "I don't know about sounds, but I've seen weird stuff there myself. Once when my family was driving back late at night from vacation, we stayed on the coastal road. It was foggy, and then all of a sudden the fog lifted and we saw Halloweenish lights."

"Halloweenish. How so?" Angel asked in a quiet voice.

"I guess I mean eerie," Gina said thoughtfully. "My dad tried to say it was northern lights, but how come the lights only flashed around the island?"

"Reflection of light and fog on water can look strange." Sam shrugged.

Dory shouted, "That's the island, right?" Then, abruptly losing her Australian accent, she added, "That place is sooo creepy."

In the autumn twilight, Sam spotted a crumbling stone mansion on the small island. It was mostly hidden by dark skeletal trees. Through the pine branches, he could see that the Sinistrus place had turrets and a wrought-iron widow's walk. He admitted to himself that the sunlight did give the surrounding water an unearthly glow.

Dory pulled the car over and parked on the soft shoulder of the highway. "Have either of you checked the mansion out?"

"No one I know has," said Gina. "The currents are treacherous off this part of the coast, *and* you're crossing breakwater."

"I think my aunt said there used to be a suspension bridge," said Angel. "But there was no point rebuilding it because *no one* goes there."

Sam believed her. Shadows on the island crawled in the dusk, snaking into dark tendrils of menace.

"You know, that island is in my nightmares sometimes." Angel gave a nervous laugh. "I dream I'm going to the island, but even as I'm dreaming I know it can't be real because I'm walking on top of the water to get there." She paused in the heavy silence and said in a lower voice, "When I get to shore, ghosts stare down at me from the tree branches." She rubbed the back of her neck nervously. "I wake up totally freaked out."

No kidding, thought Sam.

After a minute Dory broke the silence. "Well, thanks, mates, for the local tour." Then to Sam's dismay, she made a U-turn and headed back to town. She said to her friends, "I'll drop you all home."

"How about me first?" asked Sam. Their home was only half a kilometre farther up the coast.

"No can do, brother," said Dory. "I don't like making U-turns."

Hadn't she done that a few moments before? "Then let me out here."

Dory didn't slow down, saying, "I'm not supposed to stop on the highway."

"You just did!" Sam shouted in exasperation.

Gina flashed Sam a sympathetic smile.

"Don't you think you should let me out in case anyone notices you have an N licence on your windshield, and you're driving around with a car full of people?" asked Sam.

Dory kept driving.

"Technically you're only allowed one non-family member in the car," Sam reminded her.

"Oh, so suddenly we're family? Then why would I let you out?" Dory glared at him in the rear-view mirror.

"I was only thinking of you," Sam said with exaggerated concern. Angel let out an exasperated sigh, but Sam noticed Gina smirked.

"Remember *who* is in the driver's seat." Dory slowed the car. Then, just in case Sam hadn't caught her double meaning, she added, "So I call the shots."

Dory was power-tripping. She had been since she arrived and realized that staying here meant a lot more to Sam than to her. He had to figure out a way to get in the *driver's seat* before Dory drove him crazy. Sam thought about his growing lists of impossible tasks:

Make sure he made things easy for his grandmother— so easy she hardly knew she was taking care of three kids.

Work up the nerve to try out for track. That would please his father and help with the next task.

Make friends with Khallie and Blake.

And last but definitely not least—get the upper hand with Dory.

Sam considered those lofty goals as they drove back to town in the convertible—that is, until they turned off the coastal road back onto the highway. That's when Sam spotted Khallie Saran going in the opposite direction toward the coast.

It was dusk and Khallie was nowhere near her neighbourhood.

What was she doing on that lonely stretch of road?

× **4** ×

UNDER HER THUMB

T HE SUN WAS dipping into the red-streaked horizon by the time Sam and Dory approached the grey-shingled sea cottage. Dory drove her car up the winding lane along a wind-blasted bluff. The sharp briny smell of the sea and the slight taste of salt on his lips loosened a knot in Sam's chest. A knot he didn't know he had until now.

When they entered the cottage, a small person shot out of the shadows and wrapped her arms tight as a boa constrictor around Sam's waist. A smaller furry creature began weaving its way around Sam's legs.

"Hi, Sammy Sam-Sam," Molly said in delight. "I've been missing you."

"A warm hello to you too," Dory said in a sarcastic voice. She reached over to pet Molly's cat, Pix, but Pix shot out of her way.

"Hi, Dory. I'm happy to see you too," Molly said with just a touch less affection.

"Yeah, well, I'd like to say it was mutual."

Dory's insults rolled off Molly's back. Molly even managed to get a smile from Dory. That, thought Sam, was pure talent.

Sam never knew what to do with Molly's outbursts of affection. No one else loved him so... conspicuously. His father reserved his affection based on approval, and while Sam had no doubt his grandmother loved him, she wasn't the hugging type.

Awkwardly, Sam patted Molly on her shoulder. "I've, ah, missed you too."

"Dinner's in the oven." his grandmother said. "I've kept it heated so it will be dry as toast, yes? You're supposed to check in with me if you're going to be late. Isn't that the point of your fancy-dancy technology?" Sam's grandmother pointed to Dory's expensive cellphone. "You can't have your cake and eat it too."

Sam wondered why anyone would want cake if they couldn't eat it.

"It wasn't my fault," Dory said, turning her back to them and jutting her chin over her shoulder in Sam's direction. "I couldn't just leave *him* behind even though he kept me waiting, could I?"

"Sam, you know better," his grandmother frowned.

That was it. Sam couldn't take it anymore. Dory was getting away with murder. "Dory was driving around with her..."

"Is our dad checking in this week?" Dory asked sweetly. Babcia nodded. "Yes, he's calling soon."

Sam folded his hands into fists and pressed them against his thighs.

His father had set strict rules for this experiment of living with their grandmother.

Rule # 1. *Do exactly what Babcia tells you to do.* Sam and Molly tried. But Dory was a wild card. Sam knew if he said being this late wasn't his fault, it would only make things worse by breaking...

Rule # 2. *Do not force Babcia to become a referee for your arguments.*

Was arguing worth being shipped back to boarding school? Was living with an even angrier Dory after she had her licence confiscated a life worth living?

"Sorry about being late," Sam mumbled.

Dory smirked, and Sam promised himself that he'd find a way to get out from under her thumb.

THAT NIGHT AT dinner, Sam broached the subject of sea echoes with his grandmother. She was, after all, Professor Novak of the Ocean Institute.

"Babcia," Sam slurped down a gulp of milk, "has anyone at the Institute ever reported weird ocean sounds off our coast—like really weird monster echoes?" His grandmother frowned.

"Eew," Dory said, waltzing into the kitchen. "It's bad enough that I have to share a bathroom here with everyone, but I absolutely refuse to use a bathroom mirror that Sam squirted with pimple juice."

Sam's face flushed a deeper crimson than the squares on the tablecloth. The sore spot on his chin throbbed.

"What's pimple juice?" asked Molly. She dragged another chair to the table, its legs scraping against the checkered black and white tiles. "Can I have some more chicken?"

"It *isn't* dinner conversation," Babcia said brusquely.

"But this needs to be dealt with," Dory protested.

"Not at the dinner table," Babcia said in a forbidding tone that even shut Dory up. Well, almost.

Dory shoved her plate to Molly, saying, "Here, take my chicken. I'm thinking about becoming vegetarian. Could I maybe have an omelet instead, please?"

Sam's grandmother stood up from the table, went to the old-fashioned blue fridge, and brought out a jar of peanut butter and a loaf of bread. "Help yourself."

As the room went silent, Sam shoved his potatoes around with a fork, worrying how to keep Dory from ruining everything. Time was running out. Torturing him wasn't enough to keep her from getting bored.

Then he noticed Molly take a large chunk of chicken from Dory's plate and feed it to Pix, who was lurking under the table. While that wasn't specifically against any of their father's rules, the astonishment on Babcia's face told Sam they'd be lucky if she put up with them another month. His stomach tightened, leaving little room for the rest of his dinner.

"Maybe the chicken does look tasty after all," said Dory, taking back her plate and shooting Molly a surprised look at the paltry piece that was left.

With a shake of her head, Babcia turned to Sam, resuming their earlier conversation. "Attributing ocean echoes to any wild theory is nonsense, Sammy. That's the kind of fuzzy thinking some of my students show that makes me wish I did more research and less teaching."

His grandmother drummed her fingers on the table. "Stick to the facts. Unusual echoes are likely to be sound waves reflected off sunken objects, or an underwater earthquake."

His grandmother sounded like his father. Fact: Life isn't fair—you have to be nice to your half-sister no matter what. Fact: Life is hard—if this doesn't work out, it's back to boarding school until I get a permanent post.

For Sam, facts weren't very satisfying. Besides, even his grandmother, Professor Novak, couldn't know for sure that fault lines and sunken debris were the only reasons for monster echoes. There might be other explanations.

As soon as Sam had finished eating, he excused himself from the table and went to his room. He planned to read comics, but instead he fell asleep so early that by four in the morning he was wide awake. Restless, he decided to see if he could do some stargazing with his telescope.

When Sam entered the sunroom, he heard heavy padding behind him. Pix accepted a quick pat on the head before leaping onto the window ledge, where he let out a low howl. Sam went to the window and stared into the inky night. He could barely make out the treacherous rocks below, as a fog had rolled in. There'd be no stargazing. Then, out of the corner of his eye, he spotted what was bugging Pix.

For several moments, green lights danced around Croaker's Island. Then, as if someone had thrown a switch, the witchy lights extinguished into the midnight fog.

Something was out there, lurking. Sam couldn't explain how he knew that... only that he felt the island tugging him—like he was a compass needle being drawn toward the magnetic North Pole.

× 5 ×

LIKE OUT OF
A HORROR MOVIE

THE NEXT EVENING at Blake's, the sky was dark and crystal clear. Mrs. Evans ushered Sam onto the sprawling back deck overlooking the ocean. Blake was sitting in a chair at the table and staring at his laptop screen with Khallie and Owen.

"Come and look at this!" shouted Owen, a bespectacled boy.

Owen was a head shorter than Sam and Khallie. Babcia would describe him as scrawny and in need of fattening up. But his voice sounded confident when he said, "This doesn't look like a *bloop* echo."

"What's a bloop?" Khallie looked dubious. "Is that even a real word?"

"A bloop echo is a low-frequency but very loud sound wave, like the noise a gigantic animal might make," said Owen.

"If it's not a bloop, what is it?" asked Blake. "I picked up another series of sound waves today."

Khallie pointed to the wiggly lines on the laptop screen. "Yup, those are some gigantic noises," she commented, as if she'd been studying spectrograms her whole life.

Sam huddled beside Khallie to check out the laptop screen. He noticed how their shoulders brushed and that her hair smelled of strawberries.

Owen traced the spikes on the spectrogram with his finger. "I mean, this spectrograph pattern looks more like *slowdown echoes.*"

Blake flipped open the library book on ocean mysteries, and slammed his finger down on a paragraph. "Slowdowns are similar to patterns created by huge underwater aircraft."

"I knew it," said Sam. "Those echoes aren't from a giant squid, but from a top secret military weapon."

"Either way, you've got to report the echoes," Khallie told Blake.

"She's right," agreed Owen. "Those sound waves are super rare."

"That's exactly why I'm *not* reporting them." Blake shook his head. "I don't want to look like an idiot."

"Blake... might be right..." Sam reluctantly agreed. "My grandmother said the Ocean Institute hasn't recorded any unusual underwater sounds."

Owen went nose to nose with the laptop screen. "I don't know about the Institute, but you *are* reading this correctly.

You've stumbled onto unexplained echoes. Those *are* patterns of sound, very loud sound."

"The water is deep and cold here," said Khallie. "I still think colossal squids are migrating up our coast to gobble up whales."

"Cool," said Owen. "Like out of a horror movie."

"Not so cool for the whales," Khallie pointed out.

"You know a little bit too much about mysterious underwater creatures to be completely normal," Sam grinned at her.

Blake laughed, but Khallie turned red and looked away. Her hurt expression made Sam regret his joke, although neither he nor Blake had taken offence when she'd said something similar to them.

Owen fished inside his gigantic backpack. He brought out a radio set with huge antennae, and then he began unrolling wire from a spool.

Exactly like the little man who was lurking outside Blake's house the other day, Sam thought with a start.

"What are you doing?" Sam asked Owen, who was busily letting out a long length of wire across Blake's deck. Blake and Khallie turned to each other and shrugged.

"Trying to make a bigger antenna to pick up any radio signals being emitted in this area that might be bouncing off rocks," Owen said. He turned on the radio receiver he'd set up on the table beside Blake's laptop. Moments later he let out a small yelp.

"You hear a giant squid surfacing?" Khallie asked excitedly.

Owen shook his head. "Nope, but I have picked up other strange signals really close by."

"Where?" asked Sam.

"I'm guessing," Blake began, "it's..."

"Croaker's Island," said Owen. Blake and Khallie gave a knowing nod.

"People have been hearing strange noises on that island for years." Khallie lowered her head and nervously pulled on her charm bracelet, rattling the dangling silver hearts and rubies. "I get bad dreams about that creepy place."

That's what Dory's friend Angel had said. Sam wanted to ask exactly what Khallie dreamed about, but he hesitated. Was that too personal?

Blake closed his laptop with a snap. "That settles it. We've got to explore Croaker's Island."

"How?" asked Sam.

"Ah, row a boat," said Blake with a sarcastic smile.

"Will your parents let you? Those waters are dangerous." Khallie looked incredulous.

"Let me figure that out," said Blake. "Is it possible we can rig our own hydrophone and drop it off the far shore of the island? That way, we cast a wider net to pick up the echoes."

"The materials for a hydrophone wouldn't be expensive." Owen put his hand on his chin and began muttering, "I could rig a transducer that generates electricity as the water pressure changes, and sound is a pressure wave. It'll need a conical reflector to focus the signals." His voice rose in excitement. "I want to come with you when you make the drop. I'll tell my parents it's for Scouts and tag along,"

"You shouldn't lie," Sam said automatically.

"There's no way they'd let me row to that island on my own. Those currents are dangerous," Owen pointed out.

Sam shrugged. "You still shouldn't say you're at Scouts."

"If that's the case, maybe I should leave. They think I'm at Scouts now." Owen shot them a wry smile and gathered his stuff, saying, "See you later."

After Owen left, Blake rolled his eyes, but smiled. "I guess the guy is all right."

"And he's super smart," said Khallie.

"So, we're on for exploring the island?" asked Sam.

"Not *we*, you three. Count me out." Khallie stared past the deck toward the crashing sea. "That place is too spooky."

Blake coughed suddenly. "In the meantime, is anyone interested in astronomy? I've set my telescope up," he said out of the blue.

Puzzled, Sam realized Blake had suddenly switched the conversation when his mother appeared at the patio door. Sam had been so busy staring at the laptop screen, he hadn't noticed the telescope on the other side of the deck. So Sam and Blake had another thing in common. "That's a deluxe model."

Blake said, "Go for it."

"Blake, you have more company," said Mrs. Evans.

Sam turned around as an uninvited guest stepped onto the deck.

Sam's face heated up. What was *she* doing here?

× **6** ×

MARS IS IN RETROGRADE

SAM AND HIS friends stared at Dory, who'd just walked through the open patio door.

"I should bring out more refreshments." Mrs. Evans eyed the plate of crumbs on the table.

"No, thank you, Mrs. Evans. I've got to get Sammy back home to his granny."

Sam stared in horror at Dory.

Khallie gravitated toward Sam. "If you ever murder her, I'll testify on your behalf," she whispered in his ear.

"What are you kids up to?" asked Dory in her fake accent.

"We're about to look at some stars," Khallie said evenly.

"I know lots about stars. I'm a Capricorn," Dory said.

"That's astrology not astronomy." Blake arched his eyebrows.

Dory waved her hand dismissively. "It's still all about stars, mates."

"Astronomy is about constellations, not predictions," said Sam.

"Astrology covers planets too," said Dory. "Like when the moon or Mars is in retrograde. Then watch out, you're going to have a bad month."

"The moon's not a planet," Khallie pointed out.

"Whatever," Dory shrugged.

"We'd better go." Sam had to get out of there before Dory embarrassed them both... even more.

"Let me help Mrs. Evans tidy up first," Dory said primly. Gathering plates and cups, she went into the kitchen.

Frowning, Sam wondered what she was up to. With Dory he always felt like a pawn on a chessboard—moved a square and then sacrificed.

"Don't tell *anyone* about me being a stargazer." Blake glared at Sam and Khallie.

Sam was puzzled. "But stargazing is cool."

"I wish I was more like you," Blake told him, "and didn't care what people thought about me."

Sam wasn't sure if that was an insult or a compliment. He shrugged. "I care what people think, but I don't let it keep me from doing what I want, or I wouldn't like my life much."

A thoughtful expression stole over Blake's face. "I... I'm starting to get that," he said quietly. Then Sam and Blake talked about how the horizon was usually cloudy by the water, and Blake told him if he travelled a little farther inland, the sky was clearer there for stargazing.

"You guys know the new observatory at the university is holding free astronomy classes every week, right?" said Khallie. They turned to her.

"Yeah, I guess you *nerds* don't know everything," Khallie said with a smirk. "The community centre is sponsoring a star program."

The three of them looked at each other and instantly agreed they'd sign up together.

"Will your parents allow you to join a night class?" Blake asked Khallie. "Aren't they crazy strict?"

Sam didn't know what to make of the look that crossed Khallie's face as she quickly said, "I'll... tell them it's for school. I'm sure I can get extra credit."

Sam couldn't help it, but his heart took a little leap when she said she'd join them. Someone came up from behind and patted him on the head.

"That's nice this little guy's got something in common with all of you," Dory said in a sickly sweet sisterly voice. "He wants to make friends."

Blake shook his head and grinned. Sam felt the blood rush to his face and wished he could crawl under a rock. Instead, he said goodbye.

"See you tomorrow," Khallie called after him as he walked away.

Sam didn't care for the amusement in her voice.

On their drive back to the cottage, Sam said, "Okay, Dory, what's with the 'get the little guy home to his granny' crap?"

"Chill, mate," said Dory. "Your babcia, or whatever you call her, made me pick you up and..."

"She's your grandmother too," Sam reminded her. "How can you not know *babcia* is Polish for grandmother? She was born in Poland, you know."

"Right, well, I didn't, or I forgot. I mean, she has a bit of an accent, but I've only met her like three times before I got stuck here. My mother never mentioned..." Dory drifted for a second then snapped back. "Anyhow, I just saw a picture on the mantle of Blake's older brother, a college guy. His name is Colton," Dory said dreamily. "Mrs. Evans says he's nineteen, so I want to impress her with my maturity. Maybe she'll mention me to the brother," she sighed. "Colton Evans."

An idea hit Sam like a lightning bolt. "I *could* use a ride to and from astronomy classes," he said. "If *you* drive me, you can chat with Mrs. Evans in the parking lot. That would show her you're responsible and helpful."

"You've got it," Dory said. "Mercury is definitely not in retrograde over Capricorn. I'm feeling *lucky* in love."

Sam felt a little lucky himself. Dory's interest in Blake's older brother might be his ticket to keeping her happy and cooperative. If he played it right, he'd be in the driver's seat soon.

As long as he only dangled *the possibility of meeting Blake's brother* in front of Dory, what could go wrong?

× × ×

THE FIRST NIGHT of astronomy class, Sam couldn't wait for dinner to be over, even though Babcia had made thick, delicious borscht with warm bread on the side. After Dory had grumbled through the dishwashing and Sam had dried the dishes, Babcia sat at the kitchen table with her knitting.

"Look, Sammy, Babcia's making us matching sweaters," Molly chirped.

"Matching sweaters, that's... nice, Molly." Sam tried sounding enthused. Behind Babcia's back, Dory smirked before she disappeared down the hall.

"She's even made a matching green and yellow pom-pom for Pix." Molly bent over the cat sprawled under her chair and tied the pom-pom onto his cat collar.

"You need to look handsome for your new friends," Molly told Pix.

"Cat friends?" Sam asked puzzled.

Molly shook her head. "No, they're people friends. I hear kids call to him from my bedroom window. I have to get up and close the window or he'll jump out. I told him we're not allowed to play outside after dark."

Sam remembered the posters of missing cats. "Don't let Pix wander, Molly. Cats have gone missing."

Molly squealed in alarm. "Oh, no!" She lifted her cat onto her lap and hugged him tight. Pix stared longingly at the butter dish.

"Pix can't sit at the table," Babcia said firmly.

Molly released him, and he jumped onto the window ledge, trying unsuccessfully to bite off the pom-pom.

"Sam, you'd better be ready if you want a ride to the observatory." Dory breezed in after a quick visit to the bathroom with her hair piled on her head and her eyelids lined like an ancient Egyptian's.

Babcia scrutinized Dory. "Don't you look nice," she said suspiciously. "And just to drive your brother to his astronomy class?"

Sam grabbed his jacket and raced for the door before Dory could open her mouth and get them in trouble. Sam figured their grandmother wouldn't appreciate Dory being interested in a college guy, even if he was only a couple of years older than her.

"Sammy didn't say goodbye," Molly complained.

Babcia needn't have worried. Dory's grand plan of chatting with Mrs. Evans in the parking lot was for nothing. Even though they arrived early, Blake's parents had already left. Complaining every step of the way that Sam had been too slow getting ready, Dory headed for the library to do her homework rather than hang out with Sam and his friends. That was a big relief.

Sam found Blake sitting on a chair beside the giant telescope inside the circular observatory. Only three other people waited in the astronomy class—two middle-aged women who introduced themselves as Betty and Diane, and a guy who looked a little older than Dory. He mumbled his name—George—that he was in college, and that he hosted a podcast about unexplained mysteries that he hoped would go viral when he landed a big story.

Just before the class began, Khallie burst in. She looked breathless, and the circles on her eyes were even darker than before. But she greeted them with her usual cheeriness.

The door on the other side of the circular room opened, and the astronomy professor walked in. The podcast guy snickered. Sam sucked in his breath.

It was the strange little man with the bumpy face, long white hair, and thick eye-glasses.

× 7 ×

PROFESSOR
MARIGOLD

"**G**ET A LOOK at the professor," Blake said softly. "I mean, whoa."

Sam blinked his eyes. "There is something strange about him." Again he felt the hair at the nape of his neck bristle.

"Shush, you two," hissed Khallie. "How rude."

"I mean..." Sam started explaining how he'd seen the professor lurking in the bushes by Blake's house, but before he could finish, the professor looked directly at Sam. Then the professor drew himself up on his toes so he could reach the podium, adjusted his white lab coat, tucked a strand of white hair behind a hairy ear, and cleared his throat.

"Good evening, ladies and gentlemen," the man said. "I am Professor Marigold, and I hope you will enjoy tonight's thrilling journey through the stars. There are billions of stars in the sky, more than you can shake a leg at."

"Do you mean shake a stick?" asked Sam.

The ladies clapped enthusiastically, but the podcast guy snorted and muttered, "Marigold? Seriously?"

Khallie scowled at him. Sam was on her side. It didn't seem polite making fun of somebody's name, especially when they looked so... different.

Owen Chatterjee ran into the observatory, knocking over a small stand as he did so. A star globe fell to the floor with a bang and rolled along a little. He scooped it up and set it back on its stand.

"Walk much?" jeered George, who Sam figured was old enough to know better.

"I almost missed you guys until I called Sam's grandmother," Owen wheezed. He took out his puffer and inhaled before continuing, "I don't remember us saying we'd meet here."

Sam's face heated because they hadn't even thought about inviting Owen to sign up for the class with them. Dodging that subject, he gestured at Owen's Scout uniform covered in merit badges. "Let me guess. You're supposed to be at Scouts?"

"I told my parents I'm working on my astronomy badge," Owen smiled slyly. "And now I am."

Professor Marigold cleared his throat again. "You are in for a huge treat, as we have a clear night." He pressed some buttons and flicked a toggle switch on a dashboard next to the telescope. The domed ceiling of the observatory dilated and the giant telescope began rising.

The cold, sharp tang of sea air rushed in, and Khallie shivered in her thin, silky hoodie. Before Sam could offer her his jacket, Blake had ripped off his sweater and handed it to her. She smiled, and Sam could only wish that Khallie would gaze at him so gratefully.

"You should have layered up, dearie," the lady named Diane told her. "It mentions that in the brochure."

When Sam took his turn at the telescope, he drew in a sharp breath as he viewed two stars rotating around each other, a dwarf star and a nebula. Stargazing reminded Sam of how those distant lights sparked such curiosity and wonder inside him—it was a good feeling.

"This is cool." Blake took his turn by leaning from his chair and straining to see through the telescope. Without attracting too much attention, Sam shoved Blake's chair closer to the lens.

"Do you suppose anyone's looking back at us?" Khallie asked.

"The distant galaxies and stars we're looking at tonight are only rocks and dust, gas and vapour," said Professor Marigold. "No one's out there at all."

Sam didn't want to believe that for a second. Where was the mystery?

"That sounds so lonely," said Diane.

"But there are billions of planets, Professor," said Blake.

Professor Marigold waved his hand. "The delicate balance of life requires a rare mathematical symmetry. Do any of you know what the Goldilocks Zone is?"

Khallie politely raised her hand, but then only scratched her head.

Owen jumped in. "Professor Mari... ah... gold, that's where life can only exist on a planet that's close enough to the sun so it isn't frozen, but far enough away so everything on the planet doesn't burn to a crisp."

Khallie's face brightened. "I get it. You mean the story of Goldilocks and the Three Bears where the porridge is not too hot or too cold, but just right."

"Yeah," said Sam.

"That is... mostly... correct," said Professor Marigold. "And I'm sorry to report that countless planets in countless galaxies are not in the Goldilocks Zone."

"Isn't there an Earth-like planet at the right distance from its star called Kepler 186f?" Owen said matter-of-factly. "Also Planet 0.482, Sector .08, of the Sagittarius galaxy?" George, the podcast guy, did a double-take.

Sam thought the professor gave Owen an odd look.

"Professor Mari-whatever," said George, "there are so many reports of unexplained phenomena in our sky."

"That's right," Owen burst in. "And not only above. In our ocean, right off this shore we've just discovered mysterious echoes. Just ask my friends here—we've seen the spectrograms. Mysterious echoes that are unexplained, right, Blake and Sam? Khallie?"

Professor Marigold turned sharply and stared at them.

"Right?" Owen's gaze darted toward each of them.

Sam hesitated. He couldn't believe Owen had blurted out what they'd sworn to keep secret. Who else had he told? When Owen gestured for Blake to say something, Blake ignored him and stared through the telescope again. Khallie shook her head slowly, trying to warn Owen not to say any more.

For several long seconds the only sound in the observatory was the hiss of the heater trying to pump a little warmth into the icy room.

"Hey," George said. "If you know something about sea monsters, kid, that could make a cool podcast episode."

Owen finally noticed Sam's, Blake's, and Khallie's horrified expressions. "I just meant . . . life can exist in extreme conditions . . . Places where scientists thought nothing could live and . . ." Owen's voice petered out. His face went two shades redder.

Professor Marigold sighed, shook his head, and sounded almost exactly like Babcia as he said, "Please let us not get carried away with science fiction nonsense."

"Nonsense? That kid had the most interesting information tonight. The rest of this class has been a total waste of time." George got up to leave. In a parting shot he said, "I'm not going to get anything useful for my podcast."

"How rude," said Betty. Diane nodded.

Professor Marigold ignored the departing student and said brightly, "That is it for tonight's class." He pressed some switches, and the dome closed. Khallie rushed out, saying she'd better not keep anyone waiting.

Sam noticed Blake's father standing in the hallway by the open door. His hands were on a wheelchair.

"C'mon, Owen, I'm thinking your parents will be wondering why you're so long at ... Scouts." Sam tugged him outside as Blake gave him a grateful nod and waved goodbye. The professor hurried out the door.

Outside in the parking lot, Dory was in an intense conversation with the podcast host. "George, I'm telling you, mate, Australia is a total hotspot for UFO sightings. I've seen a few peculiar things in my time."

Owen's parents pulled up in a van, and Sam waved goodbye. He waited for Dory while George handed her his card. "If you ever want to do an interview for my podcast *Unexplained Phenomena,* give me a call." George crooked his eyebrow and looked hopefully at Dory. "We could even do it now if you want to."

Big mistake, thought Sam. Dory didn't fall for guys who looked that eager.

"Another time." Dory gave her twisted smile.

Yup, Sam called it.

When George left, Dory said to Sam, "Are the Evanses here yet?"

"I, ah, *think* they've gone," said Sam.

"Get in the car."

As they drove across the campus, Sam spotted several curious things. First, they drove past a series of telephone poles plastered with missing-cat posters. There seemed to be an epidemic of missing cats. He'd better warn Molly again to keep a close eye on Pix. The second curious incident was that he saw Professor Marigold enter the oceanography building, even though it was pitch dark. He knew that section of the college because he'd visited his grandmother there. What business would an astronomer have in there? The final thing he saw made him forget about the other peculiar things...

When Dory drove past the bus stop, Sam saw Khallie waiting for the bus.

"Stop the car; we should give Khallie a ride home."

Dory didn't want to back up in the middle of the street but agreed to drive around the block. But when they'd turned around and passed the bus stop, the bus had just left, its tail lights disappearing into the dark.

Why would Khallie's super-strict parents let her take a bus home so late in the evening?

× 8 ×

WE'RE NOT
FIGHTING

O N FRIDAY MORNING, Sam was making toast
for Molly and sipping a steaming mug of hot
chocolate when Dory waltzed into the kitchen
saying, "So... are you meeting up with your friends later?
I'll be the chauffeur."

"Can I come too?" asked Molly.

"It's not working out, me taking you to the observatory," said Dory. "I didn't realize there were so many
parking lots. I never spotted Mrs. Evans. But if I drive
you to Blake's, I can just hang out with his mother and
ask about Colton."

"What about me?" Molly insisted. "I want to look at
the stars."

"The astronomy class is past your bedtime," Sam told
Molly.

"That's not fair," she grumbled.

Sam turned and said to Dory, "You don't have to come with me to my friends' houses. I'm sure you'll bump into Mrs. Evans next class." It would be tricky keeping Dory cooperative, especially if she was going to hang around and embarrass him all the time. Unless... "What about that George guy?" Sam said nonchalantly. "Didn't he say he wanted to interview you? You could meet him after class."

"It's *not fair* I can't go stargazing," Molly said more loudly, tugging on Sam's sweater. Pix jumped up onto the kitchen table. Sam made a grab for him, but the cat squirmed out of his grasp.

Dory said, "George is not my type. He dresses like a dork."

"Nice values," said Sam, rolling his eyes.

"Look who's talking, brother," Dory said coolly. "Your new friends are the most popular kids in middle school. And that little girlfriend of yours is quite the fashionista."

Narrowing his eyes, Sam said, "Khallie's not my girlfriend."

"Excuse me. I mean the girlfriend of your *dreams*," Dory smirked.

"I *need* more friends," said Molly.

That wasn't why Sam liked hanging around with Khallie and Blake... was it?... Because they were popular? *I include Owen as a friend.* "I . . . don't *need* any rides from you."

"Yes, you do!"

"No, I don't!"

"Yes, you . . ."

"Don't fight!" Molly cried. "It'll be just like last holiday with you two always fighting. Stop it!"

"What's this shouting about?" Babcia entered the kitchen and quickly seized Pix, who was still on the table and lapping butter from a dish. "Bad cat!" She opened the kitchen door and tossed Pix outside.

"Don't be angry, Babcia. Everyone stop fighting," Molly began wailing. "I want Daddy. I want Pix."

"It's okay, Molly, we're not fighting," said Sam, even though the air was thick with tension.

Babcia decided to drive Molly to school, leaving Sam and Dory to work out their argument. Dory shrugged her shoulders and said, "Well, mate, I guess you don't want me giving you a ride anymore. I can't argue with that."

Sam had already missed the school bus, which Dory knew. It took almost an hour of walking before he arrived late at school.

After school, Khallie met up with Sam at his locker. "I'm going to Blake's this evening. We're playing video games. Want to come with?"

Sam smiled for the first time that day. "Sounds good."

"Ooh, I love your new charm bracelet," Andrea Kellerman gushed as she walked by. She took Khallie's arm and admired the jangling silver heart and ruby bracelet. "Is it from Blake?"

Why did that make Sam's own heart dive?

"No. My parents love giving me gifts."

"Lucky," said Andrea. She looked right through Sam as if he wasn't standing there. Khallie waved goodbye as she walked off with her friend.

Next, two of Blake's friends approached Sam. "Is it true you're seeing Blake?" asked the track team captain, Andy Chan.

Sam shouldered his backpack. "Sometimes," he said cautiously.

"Is Blake, like, walking now?" pressed Andy.

"Of course he is. I bet he's running again," answered Ravi. Ravi was a burly kid who Sam heard had already made the high school football team even though their second year at middle school had just begun. "Blake won't let that skiing accident get in his way," Ravi said with conviction. "I bet he's back on the rowing team in the spring."

"Some little bruise on his spine isn't going to stop him," agreed Andy.

Sam didn't know what to say. He just wanted to escape and catch the last school bus or he'd be stranded again—and he didn't want to walk home either.

Andy casually flipped the locker door back and forth. "It's weird he isn't back at school. My folks say his parents aren't making him do anything he doesn't want."

"I guess that's not so weird, then," Ravi shrugged. "Who would choose school? Not me."

Andy arched his eyebrows at Sam. "How come you take him his work and not any of us?" He shook his head. "Khallie isn't saying much. It's not like her to be so closed-mouthed."

Sam wished Khallie had been *more* closed-mouthed, as in not even mentioning Blake, so Sam could get out of here. He broke through the guys. "He seems good." Sam raced down the hall to catch the bus.

"If he'd moved that fast at track tryouts, he might have made the team," Sam heard Ravi say about him.

Last week after school, when the coach had set the stopwatch, it was the same old story. Sam's skin had grown clammy, his lungs squeezed shut so he couldn't catch his breath, and then he'd hesitated one second too long. He'd *almost* made the team.

"He doesn't strike me as Blake's type," Andy added.

"Told ya Blake was doin' good," said Ravi. "He'll be back in no time."

Sam had almost made it out the door when the school nurse stopped him. "Sam, I sent you home with a notice last week. We urgently need your immunization records, and we need to know if you've ever had mumps or chicken pox."

"Sorry. I guess I forgot."

"This is top priority." The nurse wagged her finger at him and made Sam wait at her desk while she phoned his house. Babcia answered the phone and promised she'd find out the information the nurse wanted. Then Sam flew for the parking lot, but the bus had just pulled away. He started walking.

× × ×

THE REST OF the day only got worse. When Sam asked Babcia for a ride to Blake's that evening, she said "Sammy, I'd like to finish this sweater. Dory can give you a ride. After all, that's why she's got the car, to help out." Babcia looped a thick strand of bright yellow wool around her knitting needle.

At dinner Dory said, "But Sam said he doesn't want a ride after all." Dory favoured Sam with a purely evil look. "So it's okay if I go to the movies with Angel and Gina, right?"

Sam mumbled how gaming at Blake's was probably cancelled anyways.

"Maybe you'd like to clean the garage instead and have no chores for Saturday," Babcia suggested.

Sam bit his lip and said, "Have a good night at the movies, Dory, and I'll get right on clearing those boxes out of the garage, Babcia," all to keep the peace. Meanwhile, he was feeling like an elastic band being wound tighter and tighter and getting ready to snap.

An hour later, Sam was moving the last set of boxes from the garage wall, where he'd discovered a dust-covered black bicycle. It was a good one—titanium and with twenty gears. He grabbed a rag and dusted off the bicycle until it shone. He stood back and gave it an admiring whistle.

"Ah, you've uncovered your father's bicycle," said Babcia, who'd come up behind Sam. "Your dad used to travel all over town on that. He said it had all the bells and whistles."

"Where?" Sam didn't see a single bell.

"I mean it's a very fancy bike. My stars, what do young people use for expressions these days?"

Sam could say, but his grandmother wouldn't be impressed.

"Sammy, your friend Blake's on the phone." His grandmother handed him the receiver. As Sam took the phone, Babcia said with a cryptic smile, "That bike should solve your transportation problems."

Sam couldn't stop grinning as he lifted the phone to his ear. "Sam," said Blake. "I can meet you tomorrow at the wharf about a half-kilometre south of Croaker's Island. Say around four. Can you make it?"

Sam stared at the shiny black bicycle. "No problem."

× **9** ×

PRIMEVAL AND
DANGEROUS

THE SKY TURNED the colour of lead as unsettled weather rolled in from the Pacific Ocean, turning the water choppy and sending waves crashing against the shore. Sam chained his bicycle to the pier. He felt a surge of excitement when he spotted Blake in the boat. An older boy was standing up to his knees in the surf, holding the boat steady in the water. Sam recognized him from the picture on Blake's mantle, the one that Dory had admired—Blake's older brother.

After a quick "hello" to Blake and Colton, Sam took off his sneakers, rolled up his jeans, and waded out to the boat.

"Owen's not coming?"

Blake shrugged his shoulders and then shook his head. Colton looked a lot like his brother, except for his tan. Sam could tell Colton spent a lot of time outdoors.

Colton rattled off instructions. "Make sure you row along the breakwater until you're near the shore. Don't cut across it too early."

Blake said, "Seriously, bro, I get enough mothering."

"Come back in one piece, that's all I ask." Colton shoved their rowboat into the crashing surf. "Or I'm in big trouble."

Blake dug the oars into the cresting waves as Sam perched on the seat at the prow. "Let me know when you want me to row," said Sam.

"Actually, this feels pretty good." Blake stretched and strained as he worked the oars in quick rhythm. He kept the boat steady and on course.

"Is that the hydrophone?" Sam gestured to a large bundle wrapped in plastic at the bottom of the boat. Behind Blake was a coil of wire.

"Khallie brought it over last night," said Blake.

"I'm surprised Owen didn't come," said Sam. "He wanted to explore the island too, and it's his equipment we're using."

Blake slowed the oars for a moment. The boat bobbed in the surf. Sighing, he said, "It's probably for the best he's not here, right? Owen tends to blab."

Sam hesitated. His stomach did a small flip as he thought how he'd be exploring creepy Croaker's Island on his own. *Blake will be close by in the boat,* he told himself. Sam shrugged. "I guess."

Blake maneuvered the rowboat smoothly across the breakwater until lapping waves pushed it closer to shore. Dark forest covered the island. They heard nothing but the steady crash of waves; not the splash of a seal or an otter, not the cry of a gull...

Hair prickled the back of Sam's neck. He tried ignoring the chill that crept up his spine when he jumped out of the boat and secured the line. Blake tossed him the triangular hydrophone.

"Owen says we should be able to pick up the radio signal from my equipment at home," said Blake. "Drop the hydrophone off the big bluff on the other side of the island. That's near where we detected the echoes."

"Will do."

"Don't take too long, or Colton will freak."

Sam slung the plastic bag over his shoulder and started hiking. He realized it would be faster cutting across the island rather than circling around to the other shore.

But that meant he'd have to walk right past Sinistrus Mansion, which lurked behind the rocks and trees like a giant pterodactyl, primeval and dangerous, ready to launch itself at its prey...

Yeah, he'd take the other route. Except the hike around the island took a lot longer than he'd anticipated. For one thing, his wet feet rubbing against his sneakers created instant blisters on both heels. When he finally he made it to the other side, he spotted the high bluff not far from an old boat dock.

Sam tried hurrying, but scaling the steep rock bluff was slow, gruelling work. Once on top of the bluff, he got on his belly, nudged as far over the edge as he dared, and looked down at the dropoff. The water off this shore darkened from flint to dark grey where the shore dropped away into a deep trench.

Sam thought there might be a cave at the bottom of this cliff just above the crashing surf. He slowly stood, swung the hydrophone on its wire like he was lassoing a runaway calf, and let the wire slide through his hands. The hydrophone dropped with a splash and sank into the darkest depths of the water.

The wind picked up and the water churned. Clouds pushed across the horizon. A storm was rolling in. He needed to get back to Blake and the boat fast, only that meant cutting past Sinistrus Mansion.

Sam hiked through a patch of arbutus trees. Their bark peeled in sheets from their tree trunks, revealing patches of raw red tree trunk as if they were wounded.

A few more metres inland, the arbutus trees gave way to thick, sharp-scented pines, and Sam's blistered sneakered feet crunched on the dried pine needles.

Sam broke through the brush.

One by one, goosebumps erupted on his arms.

✕ 10 ✕

SOMETHING SO WRONG ABOUT THAT PLACE

THE WIND SLICED through Sam's windbreaker as he moved toward Sinistrus Mansion, uneasiness digging deep into the pit of his stomach. A spiked, wrought-iron fence, like the kind that enclosed old graveyards, surrounded the mansion. Whole rusted sections of fence were missing. Farther back, jagged broken windows gaped like corpse eyes challenging anyone to look inside. Sam swallowed, half-expecting a ghost to wave out at him.

The forest encroached on the building—heavy cedar bows scraped against it, blocking most of the lingering sunlight. The wind picked up. More clouds rolled in and covered the sun. A drizzle of rain began pattering against the tree canopy. Sam sucked in his breath and moved toward a crumbling brick pathway that sprawled out from the front porch like a thin, reptilian tongue. Sam dared himself to take a look inside instead of just cutting across the property.

The bleak mansion crouched in the criss-crossing shadows like a monster lying in wait. Sam picked his way through the patchy, overgrown lawn. He climbed the front steps, used his jacket sleeve to wipe a thick layer of dust off the window, and gazed inside.

It was murky, and it took a moment for Sam's eyes to adjust to the dim light. He hadn't known what he was expecting, but the place was empty. Wallpaper was peeling from the walls in thick scales. The step rails were missing from the spiralling staircase. An old chandelier tilted dangerously from the ceiling. He'd just started to back away when he spotted newspapers spread out on the floor. Small clumps of what looked like fur were scattered on the paper. Odd. What looked like an electric razor sat on the newspaper. He hadn't expected to see that. He tried the door handle.

A high-pitched screech reverberated inside his head. He thought his eardrums would split. Chills rode up and down his spine and his heart started racing. For the life of him, Sam couldn't explain how or why, but he was scared to death. He turned and hurried down the steps. He tore across the property and jumped over the half-tipped iron fence and didn't slow down as he sped across the uneven ground.

As Sam neared the beach, his foot caught and became tangled in a trailing bramble vine, pitching him forward. As he sprawled on his hands and knees, his hand flew out and he brushed against a clump of something leathery. Pulling his arm back, he jumped up. Then he looked down at his feet and let out a sharp gasp.

By his left foot was a huge nest of *cat collars*.

What had happened to those cats who'd been wearing those collars? He thought of the clumps of fur scattered on those newspapers. An icy lump sat in his stomach.

"Hurry, man, the waves are getting choppy!" Blake shouted from the shore. "A storm's in the works."

Sam almost flew back to the boat, then fumbled with the knots and untethered the rope that secured it. He took a deep breath and swallowed, trying to calm his heart. His throat was dry. He yanked off his shoes but didn't bother rolling up his jeans as he strode into the water; the currents and undertow had grown so strong he almost fell into the crashing surf. Then he tossed in his shoes and leaped into the rowboat, tipping it a little too far port side.

"Careful!" Blake shouted, righting the boat with his oars.

"Sorry," said Sam, taking another deep breath.

"Are you okay? You're as pale as a ghost," said Blake, as he sank the oars into the water and began rowing.

Sam nodded, then turned his head and stared at the retreating island. There was something so *wrong* about that place.

"Did... did you hear any weird noises while I was on the island?" Sam grabbed onto the bench as the waves tossed the boat left and right, making him dizzy.

Blake grunted, "No," as he fought against the swelling waves. He shook his head. "I should have brought the racing boat, then we could both have rowed."

Sam noticed sweat beading on Blake's forehead. He leaned forward and said, "Hand me an oar. We still can."

"No. I can do this." Then a wave battered against the boat, leaving a pool of water at their feet. After the prow rose and dipped sharply from another huge swell, Blake handed Sam the oar.

"Just tell me what to do," said Sam as he dug into the waves.

Blake shouted, "Left, right, double-time," and "left" again.

Sam used his full body weight against the oar, fighting the treacherous currents as they crossed the breakwater. Waves lashed the side of the boat, and rain poured down, soaking them. The wind and pounding water made Sam's ears ache, and the salt spray that coated his face and lips made him thirstier. He blocked all that out as he dedicated every thought to the rhythm of rowing, and soon they neared the shore.

"Hurry!" Colton yelled from the shore as a fork of lightning lit the sky, followed immediately by a crack of thunder.

When they were almost back, Blake asked, "So, what did you mean by strange noise?"

"When I cut across the mansion property, I thought I'd check out the place—you know, just look inside a window or see if the front door opened." Sam suppressed a shudder. "But when I tried the door handle I heard such a loud screech, I thought my head would split."

"I thought I saw a flash of green light." Blake kept rowing as he looked over his shoulder. "Maybe it was the approaching storm."

"Also I saw something really strange, a bunch of cat coll..."

Colton grabbed the boat and hauled them up on the beach. He swore, and then he said, "Sorry, but you guys had me worried. Those waves are high, and the water's dangerous as it is, and..."

Blake grinned at his brother. "It was the best time I've had since..." Then he paused and Colton gave him a sharp look. Blake leaned over and pounded Sam on the shoulder. "Best time ever, maybe."

Sam had explored a creepy island, almost got scared to death, crossed treacherous breakwater rowing through a storm… He surprised himself by saying, "Yeah, me too, best time ever." He'd had a real adventure—and not the kind you ever got at boarding school or being the odd man out at home with his grandmother and sisters.

"So, when do you want to go back?"

Blake laughed, but Colton shook his head. "Not any time soon," Colton told them. "I can't take the worry."

Blake sat in the boat, waiting for something. Colton gestured at the rain-soaked Sam and said, "Maybe you need a ride back."

Instinctively, Sam knew Blake didn't want to be seen being placed in his wheelchair. "It's not like I can get any wetter." Before anyone could say anything else, Sam jumped on his bike and rode away.

It was a great bike anyway. As he rode home, though, Croaker's Island weighed heavily on his mind.

✕ 11 ✕

ZOMBIES AND GHOSTS

EVEN AFTER SAM had dried out and had dinner, he couldn't get that afternoon's adventure out of his system. The storm had passed as suddenly as it had appeared, and the night sky was clear. He fiddled with his telescope in the sunroom, turning it toward the island while his grandmother knitted and Molly teased Pix with a string of wool.

"Can I stargaze?" asked Molly. "I tried it today but only saw a bunch of seagulls."

"It helps if it's dark," said Sam.

"That's a *flock* of seagulls." Babcia's needles clicked as she knitted a very long sweater sleeve.

"Yes, Professor Babcia. Sam, can I look at a flock of stars?" Molly asked solemnly. "Will you show me Polaris and the Big Dipper?"

"How do you know about those stars?" asked Sam.

"Daddy," Molly said. "He teached me."

"*Taught* you, little one," Babcia smiled over her clicking needles.

Sam had a flash of memory of his mother and father and him on the beach, with his father pointing out stars, saying, "There's Orion's Belt, Sammy." Sam's throat grew tight. He'd forgotten about those times. His father now seemed as far away to him as those constellations.

Sam pointed through the window. "There's Polaris right there. You can't get lost if you can always find the North Star."

Molly bear-hugged Sam. "When you went away to school every year, I thought you were lost. Now that I can find Polaris, I won't ever lose you again," she said.

Babcia looked up from her knitting. Sam patted Molly lightly on the head, and was about to tilt the telescope toward the sky when the phone rang. Babcia went to the kitchen and called out, "Molly, Sam, Dory, it's your father."

With a gleeful shout, Molly raced to the phone. Sam followed more slowly. After Molly finished updating their father on her kindergarten teacher and Pix's antics and had given about twenty kisses goodbye over the phone, she handed the receiver to Sam.

"How's it going, son?" said his father.

"Good," said Sam.

"Good? As in how?" pressed his father.

Sam shrugged and realized that his father wouldn't see that. "It just is," Sam said.

"Did you make the track team?" asked his father.

"... Almost ..."

"You know what I always say, Sammy ..."

"Get back on the horse," Sam muttered.

"Maybe try out for basketball. That's how you meet friends," said his father.

Sam fiddled with the old-fashioned telephone wire on the landline. A few seconds passed in silence before his dad said, "Good to hear your voice, son. Is Dory there?"

Sam shouted, "Dory, phone!"

Dory sauntered out of her room. "Didn't you hear Babcia? It's Dad," said Sam.

Dory's lips twitched like she was hiding a smile.

Molly whispered, "Her mother *never* calls."

Sam went to get a glass of milk in the kitchen before he returned to the sunroom. Molly was backing away from the telescope. She spun around when she heard his footsteps. She looked up at him with wild eyes. "Sammy," Molly blinked back tears. "That island out there is scary."

"Why do you say that?" asked Sam.

"It has zombies and ghosts," Molly whispered.

Sam tried convincing her it must have been shadows, or maybe moonlight bouncing on the waves, but that night Molly insisted on keeping on the light in the bedroom she shared with Dory. Dory's complaints rattled down the hallway, causing their grandmother to go into their room twice, and when the arguing continued, Babcia finally allowed Molly to sleep with her.

The clock was ticking, and Sam realized with dread that his grandmother's patience with this living arrangement was running out.

✕ ✕ ✕

THE DAYS PASSED slowly until the next astronomy class. Sam couldn't wait to hear if the hydrophone he'd dropped off at Croaker's Island had shown any spectrogram echoes on Blake's laptop. He also couldn't wait to see his friends. He hardly saw Khallie now that he rode the bike instead of the school bus.

Only Babcia wouldn't allow him to ride the bike at night. *Sometimes,* Sam suddenly thought, *to get what you want, you have to give somebody what they want.* He got an idea.

He said to Dory, "Blake might want his brother to take him around at the fall fair next weekend. You could meet Colton. Maybe he's tired of the usual town girls and looking for someone more... Australian."

"Do you think so?" Dory's eyes widened.

"I'm not sure what time they're going, though. If I went to astronomy class, I could ask Blake."

"Well, hurry and get ready if you want a ride," said Dory. She flew to the bathroom to fix her makeup.

Sam wasn't lying. He'd honestly ask Blake about the fair. He doubted Blake would want to go to some lame fair, but that wouldn't be his fault. Problem solved and Dory was back on board about driving him to the observatory. It was all under control. As long as he dangled the carrot, the horse would pull the cart.

Who would have thought one of Babcia's sayings would prove useful?

× 12 ×

NOT EVEN BUGS
OR WORMS

"**H**EY, SAM!" KHALLIE called out as she raced across the observatory's parking lot. "Are you going to the fall fair?" She was out of breath as usual, like she'd hurried everywhere at a breakneck pace. She inhaled the crisp September air and added, "The theme this year is going to be pirates. Dumb, huh?"

Sam was about to agree, but he hesitated because of the excitement in her voice. "Um, are you going?"

Khallie nodded enthusiastically. "Yeah, I'm a sucker for carnivals—the fun games, the food. I even love the cheesy decorations."

"Yeah, uh, me too," said Sam.

When Sam and Khallie entered the observatory, Blake was already in his seat beside the huge telescope. Betty and Diane sat in chairs on the other side of the circular room and waved at them. George was a no-show, which was probably for the best. He was nice to Dory but not to anyone else. It was sort of embarrassing how rude he was to Professor Marigold.

Sam joined Blake. "Any new echoes show up on the spectrogram?"

Blake shook his head, looking disappointed. "No. I haven't recorded any this week."

"I bet you'll pick up an echo when we drop the hydrophone I made you off Croaker's Island!" shouted Owen, who once again came in as if he was running the last lap of a race, almost knocking over the star globe again.

"The underwater microphone's already been dropped," said Sam. "We did that on Saturday."

Owen slammed to a halt. "What?" He shook his head slowly. "Without me? Sam, is that why you never showed up to the gaming tournament you signed up for a couple of weeks ago?"

Sam had forgotten all about the tournament. So much had happened since then. He had new friends. He had a great new bike he'd been riding around all week. Then it hit him.

Blake had said, "It's probably for the best. The guy tends to blab, right?" So Owen had been purposely left behind. Sam had acted as if he'd agreed, but he didn't know Blake hadn't told Owen they were going to the island. Now

Owen looked crushed, and Khallie glared at them. Sam felt his face heat up—he hadn't asked too many questions.

Blake said smoothly, "Dude, I didn't want you getting in trouble with your parents."

Sam shrugged his shoulders and said, "We're not getting any signals anyway. You didn't miss anything."

Owen looked away from them for a second, and his throat moved as he swallowed a couple of times. "I guess. But I could have double-checked the transmitter." He blinked a couple of times. "I could make sure your receiver is working..."

"Sure, sometime," said Blake. Blake's answer was kind of vague. Owen seemed satisfied, though, and went to greet Professor Marigold as he arrived at the observatory door.

"You didn't want Owen getting in trouble? Give me a break," Khallie fumed.

"It's not like he's our frien..." Blake began.

Khallie cut him off. "Don't be a jerk, Blake. You're better than that."

Wow, that was harsh. Sam couldn't believe Khallie was laying into the guy like that, especially because he was in a wheelch...

"You're right," Blake sighed. "It's just that I don't like him telling people what we're up to."

"Are you sure it's just that?" Khallie fastened her eyes on Sam this time. "And you too, Sam. Shame on you both." Her voice dropped to a whisper as Owen came back and plopped into a chair at the end of their row. "You can't just use people," she hissed.

Professor Marigold stood at the podium, adjusting his lab coat. He fiddled with the projector's focus as he lit up the observatory ceiling with laser-projected stars.

I'm not using anyone, decided Sam. Nobody told him Owen didn't know they were dropping the hydrophone. But if he wasn't doing anything wrong, why did Sam's stomach feel funny?

"Just so I make this perfectly clear, let us begin once more by discussing the Goldilocks Zone theory about the universe," began Professor Marigold, "and how it shows the smallest and most teeny-tiny possibility of other life being highly unlikely."

"But there has to be life somewhere," said Sam raising his hand. "Even if it's bugs or worms."

The professor shook his head. "Think of the universe as a boiling cauldron of particles popping in and out of existence," he continued. "The gravitational attraction it takes to bring those particles together, the likelihood of gaseous substances solidifying and being brought into the pull of a star at just the right distance," the professor stopped and took a breath, "with just the right rotation and orbit means the possibility of life is infinitely remote, less than a nail in a haystack."

Sam shot up his hand again. "That's 'needle in a haystack.' But there are billions of stars and planets. That's got to increase the odds."

"With 95 percent of the universe known, the chance of discovering intelligent extraterrestrial life in the remaining 5 percent is unlikely," answered Professor Marigold.

"But, sir, it's the opposite." Owen frowned in puzzlement. "Only 5 percent of the universe is known; 95 percent is unknown."

Khallie raised her hand. "Like in the ocean," she added.

The professor blinked twice, and then he slowly said, "Why, yes, of course, 95 percent is unknown." He adjusted the lapels of his lab coat and stood on his tiptoes, craning his head their way. Sam did a double-take. He thought he saw the professor's large floppy ears twitch. "However, extrapolating from existing data, there can be no life whatsoever, anywhere else, no, not at all, no need to look, no need to transmit messages—no one is out there—not even bugs or worms. There's no point eating mints out of a molehill."

"Do you mean making a mountain out of a molehill?" asked Sam.

Owen shook his head slightly. He leaned over to Sam and whispered, "Something isn't right here."

Yeah, thought Sam, *the guy was terrible at old sayings even though he was from Babcia's generation.* But wait. Owen had a point. Sam's grandmother was a scientist and cast cold rational logic on things that weren't proven, and she didn't make mistakes or pretend she knew everything about the subject.

"Yeah, the guy's such a buzz-kill," whispered Blake. "He takes the romance out of the stars."

As soon as Blake mentioned romance, Khallie swung her head his way. Sam couldn't help but see the stars in her eyes.

For the rest of the lecture Sam glumly listened as the professor told them they would be viewing lifeless Jupiter's lifeless moons, Callisto and Europa, from the telescope. The observatory roof dilated, and Khallie shrugged on a snappy woollen blazer. Betty and Diane nodded in approval.

When Sam rushed past the professor to discreetly move Blake's chair into a better viewing position, he got that weird sensation again—the chill snaking up his spine and the hair bristling on his neck. Yet when he looked over his shoulder, the professor was simply pushing buttons on his desktop to rotate the telescope.

After the class was over, Owen once again mentioned to Blake that he should check the receiver on Blake's laptop.

Khallie glowered at Blake, and he swallowed, saying, "Sure, Owen, how about Saturday night?"

"But that's the opening of the fall fair," said Khallie. "Blake, Owen, why don't you come with? Sam's coming." She shot Sam a heart-melting smile, making Sam nod like a bobble-head even though his face flushed when Blake muttered something about how lame it would be.

"I'll come with you guys," Owen said eagerly. "And if you go too, Blake, I can come by your house and check the transmitter."

"I'm not going to some stupid..." Blake began.

"That's a wonderful idea," Mrs. Evans said nervously. Blake's mother and father had come into the observatory. "What a great evening out."

"No way," said Blake.

"It's time, son," said Mr. Evans. "You've stayed home long enough." Blake stopped arguing, but anger settled over his features.

"Is your other son coming?" asked Dory, who had followed in behind the Evanses. "We can bring our little sister and make it a lovely family event." Her Australian accent grew thicker and her voice sweeter than Babcia's blackberry syrup.

"That sounds nice," said Mrs. Evans. "Would you like that, Blake, to have your brother take you around?"

Sam ushered Khallie and Owen out of the observatory before Blake answered. He could tell Blake was upset. Not to mention, Sam had a bad feeling about the carnival because if Dory got near Colton, they'd either click or not. Either way, she wouldn't need Sam anymore and he'd be powerless once again. He couldn't let that happen. Maybe Khallie could help him keep those two apart.

"Hey, do you want a ride home?" Sam asked, remembering how last time he'd seen Khallie standing at the bus stop.

"Thanks, but my parents are picking me up," she said with a smile.

But when Sam and Dory drove past the bus stop, he spotted several new missing cat posters... and... Khallie boarding a bus. It was past 9:00. What were her super-strict parents thinking?

And Sam noticed for the first time that it wasn't even the bus that went through Khallie's upscale neighbour-hood. She'd boarded the bus for the coastal road...

✕ 13 ✕

ONLY TO STEP INTO
A CALAMITY

SAM HELD MOLLY'S hand as they crossed the gravel parking lot at the fall fair and stepped through the admission gate. A calliope piping out a version of "Fifteen Men on a Dead Man's Chest" drifted from the carousel. Instead of merry-go-rounds with painted ponies, there were bobbing parrots and boats. Skull-and-crossbone banners festooned the tents and lamp posts. Lanterns swayed in the constant sea breeze, lighting the night sky, and the tantalizing smell of sugar-spun candy floss made Sam's mouth water. Molly's eyes opened as wide as saucers as she took in the colourful fair.

"OMG. I saw him, Sam, and he's even hotter than his picture." Dory burst through the gate. "I think he even winked at me, but he turned a corner and disappeared."

"Who?" Sam said as if he couldn't care less, but he knew, and he immediately felt a knot in his stomach. He couldn't let those two cross paths.

"Sammy, I want to ride on a parrot," Molly chirped up. "And then a boat. And then I want to play the fishing pond game, and then I want..."

"Colton, you doofus. Quick, introduce me, because I didn't see Mrs. Evans with him. Or that poor kid in the wheelchair."

"Blake. His name is Blake," Sam said through gritted teeth.

"Sammy, I want to ride the parrot." Molly tugged his arm.

"First you want Sammy leading us to the Evanses, right," Dory said pointedly.

"I don't see them." Sam swept his eyes over the fair. So far he hadn't seen any of his friends, which was a good thing as long as Dory was in tow.

"C'mon," insisted Molly as she glared at Dory. "I don't care about meeting any Evanses."

"Why didn't you set up a meeting place with your friends?" Dory put her hands on her hips. "That's sort of a no-brainer, don't you think?"

Not when you're trying to avoid people, Sam thought to himself.

"Parrot," said Molly, tugging Sam's hand.

"Dory, I'm glad you came!" shouted Gina, as she hurried past the gate and joined them. "I was supposed to meet Angel Chan outside, but she didn't show and I already paid for my ticket." Gina pouted. "I was hoping to run into Dane as well, but he's also a no-show."

"Parrot." Molly tugged harder.

"Well, no point in hanging around here," Dory said, giving Sam a look of menace. She said to Gina, "I'm supposed to be looking like I'm at a family event, so just in case, Molly, I'll take you to the carousel while *Sam* searches for his friends. Right?" She narrowed her eyes at Sam until her demon eyebrows almost met.

Dory grabbed Molly's hand, and as they walked away, Molly gave Sam a beseeching look. Sam shrugged his shoulders and then strolled along the fairway for quite a while, crisscrossing in and out of the booths and tents on the grounds. The fall fair was crowded with townspeople, but he hadn't met up with either of his friends. He spotted Andy and Ravi at the game tent, tossing balls and knocking down pins. Beside Andy, Andrea carried a giant stuffed turtle and shouted, "Win me the pirate's chest!"

When Sam walked by them she glanced at him curiously, as Ravi leaned over and said to her, "Yeah, I heard he's been hanging out at Blake's."

"Want to join us?" asked Andrea.

Sam was confused. Had he suddenly become visible? Maybe she liked Babcia's latest sweater creation? He looked down at his striped sweater—nope, not likely. He shook his head. "Ah, maybe later." He wanted to find Khallie and Blake.

As Sam passed the hot dog stand, his stomach growled even though Babcia had made them eat dinner so they wouldn't stuff themselves with sulphites and sodium. He turned a corner and ran straight into Owen.

Owen's bag of popcorn tumbled to the ground, liberating the white puffed kernels onto the sawdust fairway. "Oops, sorry. I had my eyes closed. Hi, Sam."

"And why did you have your eyes closed?" Sam stooped to pick up the empty bag and hand it back to Owen.

Owen flushed. "I, uh, I was visualizing the spectrograms on Blake's laptop."

"There have been more echoes?" Sam's voice squeaked in excitement. His voice had been doing that lately, and it was annoying. Deliberately lowering his tone, he said, "I mean, are you talking about new echoes?"

"Yeah, a bunch of new echoes. I think they're slow-downs. What if you're right, Sam? What if they're echoes of a secret military project?"

"Not so loud..." Sam warned, but Owen wasn't listening and his eyes were closed again.

Owen shook his head. "You see, the echoes are only appearing on the transmitter I rigged. I'm thinking maybe we're the only ones picking up the signals because nobody knows about our hydrophone. I checked the audio feed from the Ocean Institute and it shows only static. It's like someone's blocking the transmissions from the other hydrophones and trying to keep the echoes a secret."

Sam got a weird flashback of Professor Marigold going into the Ocean Institute when it was closed up for the night.

"So that's why I think it's a *secret weapon* and not giant squids. If it was giant squids, the press would be all over that."

Sam noticed that Andy, Andrea, and Ravi had stopped talking and were looking their way. "Owen, shh. I'm begging you."

But Owen was so focused, he didn't notice anything or anyone else. "The echoes always spike in the evening at the same time, and the echoes are super sharp, so like I said, it can't be a giant squid or even a bunch of giant squids. But Blake isn't wrong. Those aren't phantom echoes, they're the real thing."

"Ooh, ghostly echoes? I bet it's not giant squids coming to shore to eat our town," Andy said sarcastically. "I think it's Godzilla. His footsteps would make a pretty loud noise."

Andrea and Ravi burst out laughing.

Blake had been right—they couldn't be blabbing this around for all sorts of reasons. The biggest reason right now was not to be a laughing stock. Sam grabbed Owen's arm and dragged him farther down the fairway.

"Owen, we can't let other people know what we're doing until we have more information."

Finally Owen stopped babbling. He looked at Sam's exasperated expression. "Did I do something wrong?"

"I've been all over the fairground and your friends aren't here." Dory and Gina stepped from the shadows with Molly in tow.

"My stomach hurts," complained Molly. She leaned over and barfed a rainbow all over Dory's shoes.

"Gross!" Dory gagged.

Gina stared at Dory's vomit-splattered shoes. "I told you not to let her eat two hot dogs and blue candy floss and drink an orange pop before riding the Scrambler."

"Eew, eew, eew." Dory poured her own soft drink over her shoes, trying to rinse them off.

"I don't feel good," whimpered Molly.

"We're out of here," Dory said to Molly. "And you'd better lean out the window all the way home. No puking in my car."

"You're not used to little kids, are you?" said Gina.

Molly clutched her stomach as Dory kicked off her own shoes. Owen dumped the last of his popcorn and handed her his empty popcorn bag which she then used to pick up her shoes. She stood in her bare feet for a moment, wiggling her toes in the sawdust and frowning. Then she stomped off.

"This night has been a bust," said Gina, before following Dory and Molly out of the fairground.

Sam stared after them. "I'd better go too, if I want a ride."

"I can take you back," volunteered Owen. "My parents are picking me up later in the parking lot."

"Right, you already went to Blake's. I thought he was supposed to come to the carnival," said Sam.

Owen shook his head. "He refused and his parents didn't make him. And Khallie didn't come by like she said she would." Owen gave Sam a serious stare. "Have you noticed no one makes Blake do anything he doesn't want to except for Khallie? She doesn't let him off the hook."

Owen was right. "What happened to Khallie?" asked Sam. "She was looking forward to the fair. This was her idea."

Owen shrugged. "She was going to meet with us first. Blake figured her parents didn't allow her." He leaned over and whispered, "People say they don't allow her to do a lot of stuff."

Except take buses down random roads late at night... unless she got grounded for doing just that. Sam hoped everything was all right. He and Owen lingered a while longer and tried a few video games at the arcade section of the fair, but his heart wasn't in it. Gina was right. This evening had been a bust.

After Owen's parents kindly drove out of their way to drop Sam off, he waved goodbye and headed inside his house...

Only to step into a calamity.

Every cupboard and closet had been opened and the entire contents scattered on the floor. Molly was howling for her cat, and Babcia and even Dory were trying to calm her down.

"What happened?" Sam stared at the disarray of brooms and coats and pots.

"Pix is missing!" Tears streamed down Molly's face.

"I'm sure he just went outside for a little walk," soothed Babcia.

"He's probably hiding under the couch laughing at us," grouched Dory.

"No. No. No. He's gone," Molly gulped between sobs. "I forgot to close my bedroom window, and those people came and called for him."

Molly wiped her glistening eyes and stared straight at Sam. "I think they're the zombie people." Then she began wailing again.

✕ 14 ✕

RACING
AGAINST TIME

MOLLY STAYED UP half the night, repeatedly opening the back door and calling for her lost cat. Then she'd sob when Pix didn't appear. Reassurances from Sam and Babcia that there was no such thing as zombie people who stole cats couldn't calm her. When Molly became so exhausted that she collapsed onto the couch in a miserable whimpering heap, she finally fell asleep, and then Babcia carried her to bed.

"Zombie people stole her cat. Jeez, what an annoying imagination." Dory shot Sam a scowl as if that was somehow his fault. She yawned and rubbed her eyes. "Still, something might have got her stupid cat, poor kid." Then, sighing heavily, Dory dragged her chair from the table, walked to the back door, and opened it one more time. Chilly night air crept in. She softly called, "Pix, please come home, you silly thing. Please."

Sam was half-frozen by the time she came back in; shaking her head, Dory shrugged her shoulders and went to bed.

Sam went to his room too, but he only lay on his bed and waited there until everyone else was fast asleep. He didn't have to wait long. Babcia and Dory had been falling-down drowsy. Sam, on the other hand, was as alert as if he'd drunk a bucket of power drinks.

Sam knew there was no such thing as zombie people luring cats away, but he had an idea about what *might* have happened to Pix. He never did have the chance to mention to his friends the tangled nest of cat collars he'd seen on Croaker's Island when he was running away from Sinistrus Mansion.

Quietly, Sam slipped out of his bed and put on his jacket. Changing into his pajamas had never been an option. He crept out the back door, went to the garage, and got out his bicycle. Once he'd ridden down the bluff, he switched on the bike's headlight and made his way to Blake's.

Sam rode on a hunch and a shaky plan A. There was no plan B.

When Sam reached Blake's house, he stashed his bike beside the hedge and looked up at the night sky. Stars glittered in the cool night air. He spotted the pinprick of red that was Mars. There hadn't been that many clear nights since Sam had moved here. His hunch was that Blake wouldn't let the opportunity of a brilliant night sky slip away. He rounded the side of the house and stood by the stairs that led up to the Evanses' sprawling deck, which reached over the cliff. Sure enough, he spotted a blond head glued to the lens of a telescope.

"Blake," Sam rasped, trying to whisper loudly. "Blake."

If he called any louder he'd wake the whole family. Sam grabbed a handful of small rocks and threw them on the deck. Blake's head turned. Then his head moved from the telescope, and Sam could hear something roll across the deck.

"Blake," he rasped once more. "It's Sam."

Blake peered over the gate of the deck. "Come on up."

Sam climbed the stairs, and Blake opened the gate. Sam leaned forward, trying not to stand over Blake. This was the first time Sam had seen him in his wheelchair. *It's not much different than sitting in a regular chair*, Sam thought, *only more convenient for him.*

"This better be good," Blake said.

Sam launched into the woeful tale of Molly's missing cat, and how she thought her cat had strange friends who lured him away. Then he told Blake about the cat collars he'd spotted on Croaker's Island.

"There's no way zombies stole your sister's cat."

"Kind of goes without saying," agreed Sam. "But someone is bringing all those missing cats to the island, and I think Pix might have met the same diabolical fate." Sam punched his fists together.

"I've never believed that the island is haunted," Blake added thoughtfully. "Or at least, I mean, I don't believe in ghosts."

Sam shrugged his shoulders. He was more the type to believe in undiscovered sea monsters or super-secret conspiracies than mumbo-jumbo supernatural stuff. "But..."

"Yeah, I know," Blake cut in. "When it comes down to Croaker's Island, there's always a *but*."

"And if Molly's cat has been taken there," Sam half-whispered, "I can't leave him another minute."

"Why did you come here?" Blake stared at Sam expectantly.

"I need your boat. I have to row to the island and find Pix." Those words came easily, but Sam's heart hammered out each one.

"That's not going to happen." Blake rolled back and forth in his chair. "You can't navigate those waters, at least not yet. And how would you search the island on your own?"

Sam couldn't think of details right now. He just knew he had to get to that island and save Molly's cat. He hadn't seen any live cats on Croaker's Island—only empty cat collars. Waiting even a few hours meant Pix would become the latest cat poster on the street. He shrugged. "I don't have a plan B."

"Wait here a sec," said Blake, and he rolled to the sliding door, opened it, and went inside the house. Sam noticed for the first time that a small ramp had been built so Blake could easily roll in and out, not to mention an outdoor elevator against the back of the house.

Sam shivered as he waited on the deck, afraid to leave the shadows in case one of the Evanses looked out a window. He gazed up at the sky and spotted Orion's Belt. This would have been a great night if he'd only stayed home and set up his own telescope for stargazing. It was never going to be a perfect night at the carnival, what with him riding damage control with Dory at the fall fair, but he hadn't expected it to turn out this badly.

The patio door slid open. Blake stuck his head out. "Okay, meet me at the wharf. I'll still row. My brother says we need one more man: one to stay in the boat, and two to search the island. He'll stay on shore with a spotlight so we can navigate back, and he's also bringing a rescue kayak in case there's trouble."

Sam wondered if Colton meant trouble in the water or trouble on the island.

"I've already texted Owen. Can you double him on your bike?"

"How did you know he'd still be awake?"

Blake arched his eyebrows and then smirked. "There isn't a guy in town over eleven who goes to bed earlier than 2:00 a.m. on a weekend. Even my brother is up playing video games."

Blake handed Sam a hastily scribbled address. "Owen will be waiting outside." Then Blake frowned. "I'd... give you both a ride... but..."

He doesn't want us to see his brother lift him into the boat. "It's cool," said Sam. "This is an excellent plan B."

On his bike, Sam began racing against the night sky, racing against time.

Owen was waiting for Sam behind the tree in his yard. Sam would have ridden right past, but Owen waved a flashlight. *Good thinking,* Sam thought. They'd need a flashlight to search the island. He hadn't brought any equipment. He'd just jumped onto his bike the first second he could. There was something to that Scout stuff. Owen was always prepared.

"Climb aboard." Sam waited for Owen to scramble onto the back of his bike. Owen adjusted the gigantic pack on his back. "I brought extra flashlights, a blanket, granola bars, water, and a set of walkie-talkies I built."

"Good thinking," said Sam.

"And my inhaler and some antihistamine."

"Antihistamine?"

"I have asthma and I'm allergic to cats."

Sam's heart lightened hearing Owen believed they'd find Pix. He rode off easily. Even with Owen's equipment, Sam had so much adrenaline pumping through him that it felt like Owen weighed hardly anything at all.

Sam rode his bike along the deserted coastal road. They sailed under the night sky as waves broke against the beach in a steady rhythm against the shoreline.

The sea was quiet, almost smooth, reflecting the moonlight like a dark and sinister crystal ball.

× 15 ×

OUT OF THE FRYING PAN INTO THE FIRE

WHEN SAM AND OWEN reached the wharf, Blake was already sitting in the bobbing boat, gentle waves lapping against its hull. Colton stood shivering, ankle deep in the water, holding the boat. "Stash your bike inside the van," Colton called to them. "Bring the pet carrying case in the back if we... for when we find your cat."

Sam stashed the bike and Owen grabbed the case. "Whoa!" Owen doubled over as he hauled out the pet carrier. He dropped it on the ground.

Sam gave him a hand carrying it to the boat. "This case looks like it would carry a hundred pound dog." Blake stowed it as they jumped in.

Sam would row in the front, and Blake would call directions and row in the back. Owen sat in the middle, fiddling with the huge carrying case. "Sorry you don't have much room," Colton said, noticing Owen trying to place the gigantic pet case on his lap when it didn't fit in the boat. He looked at Sam. "Your cat might be freaked going in a rowboat," he explained, "and that's the only pet case we had in the basement. We used to have a Rottweiler."

"Good old Raptor," Blake said wistfully. "Hey, did I tell you I detected half a dozen slowdown echoes tonight, right around the island?"

"What? That's... incredible..." Owen scratched his head. "I hope my transmitter isn't creating doppelganger echoes."

"Did the waves on the spectrogram look identical?" asked Sam. That would mean the echoes were not measuring correctly.

Blake shook his head. "No, I checked for that. So it's not doppelganger echoes. But they're all loud." Blake craned his head over the boat as he stared into the black sea. "Something is out there. I can feel it in my bones."

"You guys and your crazy theories," Colton said half-laughingly. But he peered closely at the black and forbidding water as he pushed them off into the still, dark night.

As they rowed toward the island, Sam fought off images of long tentacles pushing through the waves and wrapping around the boat's hull, tugging it under and into a gaping, tooth-ridden maw. *Those echoes can't be giant squids*, he told himself.

Then another picture replaced it, one of a kraken emerging from the water, lurching toward them with moonlight glistening on its long scaly neck. The giant head would lunge at them, its gaping mouth revealing rows of razor-sharp shark teeth.

"Large animals would be bloop echoes, not slowdowns," Sam muttered to himself.

The hull of the boat scraped against something and someone yelped—maybe it was Sam. Actually, maybe all of them yelped.

"What. Was. That." Owen sputtered.

Blake dug the oars into the water. There was a metallic clang. Then he pushed off as he steered the boat left. "Weird." He shook his head slowly.

Sam grabbed Owen's flashlight and shone it against the water. Something spiny lurked beneath the waves... or did it? A series of bubbles shot up, and whatever it was sank deep below the surface.

"Tell me it's not a squid. Seriously," Blake said, "or I'm turning around now."

"Whatever it is, it's made of metal. Maybe it's a sunken bridge," Sam thought suddenly. "Angel Chan said there used to be a suspension bridge to the island that sank."

"How come it moves up and down?" asked Blake.

"Waves and tides?" Sam shrugged his shoulders.

Owen shook his head. "Maybe, but..."

"Creepy. It's up to you two. Do you want me to keep rowing or go back?" Blake held his oar just outside the boat.

"What Sam wants," said Owen.

"Keep going," Sam said grimly. As he saw it, there was no choice. Pix still needed rescuing. They dug in their oars.

When they reached the rocky shore, Sam and Owen pulled off their shoes and jumped into water so icy that Sam lost all feeling in his toes, which almost made it bearable stepping on the rocks as he waded to shore. He sat the carrying case on the sand and looped a rope around a branch. Sam fiddled with the rope, trying to tie the right knot.

"Allow me," Owen said between chattering teeth. He deftly made a double sailor's knot. "I have my Scout's badge in seamanship," he added proudly.

Sam rubbed the circulation back into his legs. "Check the walkie-talkies," he suggested.

Owen swung his pack around and pulled out his walkie-talkie. He switched it on and static filled the air. "Testing, testing. Blake, please come in. Roger."

More static and Blake cut back. "Ah, yeah, sure. Um, roger."

"Owen over and out." There was another burst of static.

That's when it occurred to Sam that the steady lap of waves and burst of static were the only sounds he could hear. Not the hoot of an owl, the bark of a seal, or even the splash of an otter. He swallowed and stared at the overgrown trail that led to the house. By day this place looked bad enough, but by night it was positively menacing.

It didn't help that they'd hit that weird object rowing over here. Was it all somehow linked?

"Let's go," Sam said before his courage failed him. He held out his hand and Owen passed him a flashlight. They started tentatively along the trail.

"Wait." Sam held his arm out. He flashed his light near the mound of cat collars. Sitting on top of the pile of cat collars was one with a green and yellow pom-pom.

Sam's fear evaporated. He and Owen raced down the path, stumbling over tree roots and rocks.

× 16 ×

A MAD SCIENTIST'S
LABORATORY

SINISTRUS MANSION LOOMED ahead, dark and sprawling with its foreboding turrets, broken half-hung shutters, and rusted iron railings. The old building would give *any* haunted mansion in *any* horror movie a total run for its money.

"I wouldn't want to visit here even in my nightmares," whispered Owen.

That twigged a half-memory, but Sam needed to concentrate on the task at hand. "I think there's some kind of alarm on the door," he said, remembering his previous visit and the ear-splitting screeching. "Maybe we should try and crawl through a broken window. I noticed one at the side of the house."

"Crawl through a broken window?" Owen gulped. "Nobody said anything about breaking in... or exploring inside that place... Do... do you believe in ghosts?"

Sam shrugged. He could believe almost anything once he set foot on this island. "I think Pix might be in the house, so that's where I have to go. You can wait outside if you want." Sam tripped over a tree root. "But shine the flashlight through the window. I'm going to need all the light I can get."

"No." Owen took in a deep breath. "I've got your back. Lead on." His hand trembled as he held the flashlight, and the cone of light bobbed against a tree trunk. But he didn't back away, which made Sam think Owen also deserved a Scout badge for bravery.

They crossed the overgrown lawn, wet grass, and long weeds swiping at their pant legs, and pushed through blackberry brambles at the side of the house below the gaping, shattered window. A thorn left a nasty scratch on Sam's hand.

"There's a really weird smell inside." Owen held his nose between two fingers.

That was an understatement. An oily odour hung in the air—part sulphurous, making Sam think of a science lab, part rotting seaweed. His heart started racing. Sam held the flashlight between his teeth as he swept away some of the broken glass and boosted himself onto the window-sill. Then he scrambled through the window and tumbled lightly onto the floor. He turned around, took Owen's flashlight, and then grabbed the shorter boy's hand and hoisted him up and through the window.

"What a dump." Owen sneezed.

"Are your allergies picking up a nearby cat?" whispered Sam.

Owen shook his head. "I don't know because I'm allergic to dust too." Static snapped inside Owen's pack. He unzipped it, reached in, and took out his walkie-talkie. "Blake? Come in, Blake. Roger?"

"Blake here, guys. We must have scraped the hull worse than I thought. A little water is seeping into the boat. Not much, but I'd hurry."

"Is that a roger?" asked Owen.

"Ah, yeah, I mean," with a sigh, "roger."

"And roger that, over and out." Owen shoved the walkie-talkie back in his pack. "You heard Blake, there's not much time."

Sam hoped he was right about where Pix was, because there was a lot of island to search with the clock ticking. He moved toward the front of the house, leaving a trail of footprints on the dusty floor. The newspapers by the front door were covered in more clumps of fur, including orange and white fluff. Sam swallowed. His eyes swept the cavernous room.

"Ah-choo!" thundered Owen. "Ah-choo!"

Owen backed up and grabbed a door handle under the staircase to brace himself against his next sneeze. A door pushed open. Sam hurried across the floor and shone the flashlight inside the opening. Steps led into a cellar. Was that another tuft of cat hair? Tentatively, Sam tested the first decrepit-looking wooden step. It *felt* firm enough. Slowly he crept down the next few stairs.

"Oh, no, we don't," Owen whispered behind him. "Haven't you ever watched a horror movie? People who go down dark staircases never come back." Another sneeze interrupted.

"C'mon. According to your allergies, we're close to cats... or a mountain of dust." Before Sam could worry about what might be waiting at the bottom, he hurried down the rest of the staircase.

That's where it all got strange.

The dark dank cellar ended abruptly. A short precision-cut stone tunnel led to a longer stone-cut staircase and into a huge, deep cavern.

Their flashlights illuminated rock walls and a stone floor that spread beneath Sinistrus Mansion. It might even lead out to sea caves. That would explain why Sam could smell seaweed. It was pungently briny down here. Suddenly Sam remembered that when he'd dropped Owen's hydrophone off the sea cliff, it had looked like there were caves under the island cliffs.

Stainless steel tables, dangling pendant lamps, and tall metal cabinets were scattered across the cavern floor. Metal shelves lined the walls. The equipment reminded Sam of...

"It looks like we stumbled into a mad scientist's laboratory," Owen said in a hushed voice.

Exactly. Sam expected to see Frankenstein's monster lying on one of those tables. He swallowed again. "But it's all dusty; this place looks like it hasn't been used in years."

"Except there." Owen pointed to several tables shoved against the wall close to the stairs, only a couple of arms' lengths away. "Those tables, shelves, and cabinet aren't dusty." They shone with a silver metallic glint in their flashlight beams. On one table was a large cage covered in a grey moth-eaten blanket.

"There," Owen stifled a series of sneezes. "Cats."

Sam ran to the table and then hesitated. When he lifted the blanket, what would he find? "I'm afraid Molly's cat might be dead."

"And if you leave the cage covered, your cat's not alive or dead," said Owen.

"Huh?"

"Never mind. It's called Schrödinger's Cat. We've got to hurry, remember. The boat's leaking." Owen let out another sneeze.

Sam pulled off the blanket. Four cats lay at the bottom of the cage—one black, one Siamese, one tabby, and one *orange and white and fluffy*.

"Pix?" Sam put his hand on Molly's kitty. He was warm. Not dead. The other cats were alive as well, but they'd been drugged or something because they were all in a deep sleep.

"AH-CHOOOOOOO!!!" Owen's sneeze echoed around the cavern.

Florescent lights on the ceiling buzzed on and a high-pitched screech pierced Sam's brain. He couldn't decide if it was outside or inside his head. It didn't matter. It made his skull rattle like a maraca and his blood curdle. Sam and Owen hoisted the cage. Sam shouted over the screeching in his ears. "Run!"

He didn't have to tell Owen twice.

They lurched up the stairs at breakneck speed, Sam climbing backwards and pulling the cage, and Owen pushing from behind. By the time they made it through the front door of Sinistrus Mansion a noxious vapour was pouring out of the house. The witch-green fog wove itself around the mansion and up into the trees. It was sour and acidic, and one whiff made it seem like two hearts were pounding in Sam's chest.

"Here." Owen pulled a rope from his pack tied it to the cage so they could tow the heavy cage like a sled. "Whaaaa... whaaat's that?"

Owen pointed wildly to a large pine tree's swooping branches. Then he reached into his pocket, grabbed his inhaler, and sucked in several deep breaths.

Sam shone his flashlight. Among the shadowy branches perched two white owls. There was something very wrong with those owls. They were large. Bigger than a turkey. That wasn't the peculiar part, though.

The owls didn't stay the same shape: their lines sharpened and then distorted as if they were behind a camera lens Sam was trying to focus. And their eyes! Black pits of gaping horror stared at Sam. His heart pounded more against his rib cage. *Molly's ghosts*, he thought. *This is what she saw.* Owen screamed. Or maybe it was Sam. He couldn't tell.

The boys pounded the ground as they raced back to the boat, unmindful of the tearing branches, tree roots, and shrubs in their way. Sweat poured down Sam's forehead, getting in his eyes as he dragged the cage behind him. As they broke through the brush and the ground beneath them turned soft and sandy, some of Sam's terror subsided.

Owen gasped for air and Sam waited for him to catch his breath. Once more Owen tugged at his inhaler. "Okay, I'm good to go."

"What do you think that was?" Sam said carefully. "Not owls."

"You know, I'm thinking maybe something in those lab gases created a fog that made us hallucinate," said Owen. "Remember the peculiar odour?"

That made sense. They got confused because of the fog. Or maybe the fog distorted the owls. Sam's pulse stopped pounding in his brain as they broke through the scrub and climbed down to the sandy shore.

Blake's boat bobbed softly against the glassy water. The moon shone brightly, making everything look safer. Owen had untied the rope and begun wading into the water. "C'mon, Sam."

Pix would be okay; they'd get him checked out in the pet hospital. But still, what kind of person would steal people's cats and take them to the mansion for some kind of experiment? Who could do such a terrible thing?

Sam took a deep breath. He placed the cage down for a second next to the pile of abandoned cat collars and wiped his face. He reached over to grab Pix's green and yellow pom-pommed collar.

There, sparkling in the moonlight, caught on a branch was what at first looked like a Christmas ornament. Sam reached out and picked the shiny chain off the branch. It was a silver charm bracelet with silver hearts and ruby stones.

Khallie's bracelet!

× 17 ×

KHALLIE SARAN
IS HIDING SOMETHING

WHAT WAS KHALLIE'S bracelet doing on the island? That thought rolled over and over in Sam's head as he rowed with Blake and Croaker's Island receded into the night. He wanted to show the bracelet to Khallie and ask her how she'd lost it before he mentioned it to anyone else.

Blake had stuffed an extra life jacket against a hair-thin crack in the fibreglass hull. "Colton's gonna kill me for this," he said gesturing to the leak. "And if we sink before we reach the shore, he'll kill me twice."

Owen used a small bucket to scoop water out as fast as it made it back in. Blake shouted for Sam to bear starboard to avoid the area that had scraped the hull. When they reached the shore, Blake tossed the rope to Colton and he pulled them onto the beach. Blake quickly started explaining the leak. He was right. Colton wasn't pleased.

"How could you not come straight back?" Colton shouted. "You're not stupid. Or I thought you weren't. You know how dangerous that was."

"I didn't notice the leak until Sam and Owen were on the island. Was I just supposed to leave them there?"

"No, you should have called them back and returned right away. I'm not Mom and Dad who let you get away with murder. I should kick your…"

While they argued, Sam opened the cage and checked on the cats.

"You might want to keep that lid closed," suggested Owen. "It won't be fun wrangling four terrified cats if they wake up and leap out of the cage." He stifled a sneeze.

As Sam closed the cage, Pix snored and rolled over. The back of Pix's neck had been shaved, and there were three deep scratches. He'd seen those kind of scratches before. He leaned over and pulled what looked like a tiny black tick poking out of one of the scratches. He knew a tick could burrow deeper, but when he flicked it with his nail, it had come out easily. Then he noticed the other cats had the same marks. He checked their skin and found they each had a tick. When Sam had removed the last tick, Pix and the black cat started squawking in an irritating whine. Sam gently closed the lid. "Sorry, guys. You'd better stay locked tight. It's for the best right now."

He handed the cage to Colton. "I think the cats are okay. We can drop the others off at the rescue place. It should be easy to find the owners with all the cat posters in town."

"Did those ticks make them sleepy?" Blake looked puzzled.

Sam shrugged. "I guess."

"Did you keep one to show a vet?" asked Owen.

"No," said Sam. "I flicked them in the water before they could burrow into something else—like my arm." The cats started howling in a chorus of horrible harmony.

"They sound fully awake now," said Colton.

Once more Colton offered them a ride, and once more the expression on Blake's face made Sam decline. Colton and Blake were taking the cats to the rescue shelter, and then they were going to file a police report about the cats being stolen, so they'd be pretty late getting back. Sam might as well cycle Owen home.

"The cops might be interested in your story about some kind of underground cavern and lab at Sinistrus Mansion," Blake told Sam.

"See you in astronomy class," Owen chirped as he climbed on Sam's bike, Pix wriggling in his pack. They took off for home. After Sam dropped Owen off, he kept the pack and rode as Pix writhed inside it, banging against Sam's back.

"We'll be home soon," Sam promised. "Hold on a little longer, poor little guy." As he rode, Sam thought about the night. He liked a good adventure, especially one with real thrills and chills.

However, he decided he wasn't interested in revisiting Croaker's Island anytime soon—as in, probably never.

× × ×

THE NEXT MORNING, after Sam had received ten thousand hugs from Molly and Pix had enjoyed a hero's welcome (even though Sam was the one who rescued him), Sam dodged Babcia's questions by saying he'd got up super early to search on his bike for Pix and had found him up the coast—all of which was true. There was no need to mention early was 2:00 a.m. and where on the coast he'd been out riding. Dory favoured him with a piercing gaze, but she didn't ask any questions—fortunately.

On Monday at Seacrest Middle School, Sam waited for Khallie Saran at her locker. As she approached, she waved brightly to Sam.

"Looking forward to astronomy class? I sure am." She smiled.

"You can go? Aren't you grounded?"

Khallie looked puzzled. "Me, no, why do you ask?" She swung her locker door open.

"You didn't show up at the carnival," Sam said.

"Yeah, I fell asleep on the couch and didn't wake up until about one o'clock in the morning." She looked disappointed. "Apparently Blake and Owen and other kids called me, but I didn't even hear my phone."

The school bell rang and Khallie scooped up a textbook from her shelf. "See you later?"

"Wait." Sam reached into his pocket and handed Khallie her silver heart and ruby charm bracelet. "Did you lose this somewhere?"

Khallie reached for her bracelet, placed it on her wrist, and gazed at it thoughtfully. "I guess. I mean I looked for it on my dresser this morning, but I thought I'd just misplaced it." She looked at Sam. "Where'd you find it?"

"On Croaker's Island."

Khallie's eyes widened. She shook her head and kept looking at her bracelet. When she looked back at Sam, it was straight past him over his shoulder, avoiding his gaze. "Th... thank you."

"So you've never been to Croaker's Island?"

Khallie shook her head. "Like I said, no, and you shouldn't have gone there either. Everybody knows there's something wrong with that place."

"Oh, I believe that," said Sam. Then Khallie rushed off to class, leaving Sam standing in the hall. The second bell rang, and Sam knew he'd get a late slip—and he hadn't even handed his medical records to the nurse yet. Babcia had made him promise to do it first thing.

"I don't know why the nurse is so adamant about this," Babcia had complained. "I had to have your father send it, and that's not easy when he's deployed away from his base. But she phoned daily and was adamant even though you're up to date in all your immunizations."

Except, at the moment, Sam couldn't move.

Fact: Khallie had slept through the whole fall fair when a bunch more cats went missing.

Fact: Khallie lost her bracelet.

Fact: Some crazy cat stealer found it and dropped it on Croaker's Island.

His problem of putting one and one and one together was that he didn't think, in this case, it equalled three. Instead, he could only think of one question.

What was Khallie Saran hiding?

The tardy bell rang, and he rushed for the nurse's office with his immunization records. The nurse's office was empty, but the secretary told Sam to put his records on her desk. He didn't mean to snoop, but in a small pile on the corner of her desk were yellow medical folders. The top one had Angel Chan's name on it. Dane Parsons, Gina's friend, was the name on the second file. He flipped through a few more files and didn't recognize any names, but he guessed they were high schoolers like Dane and Angel.

Sam didn't open any files or look inside. That would just be wrong. But he also didn't have to. Each file had a fluorescent green sticky note on top. Each note stated: had measles; had mumps; had whooping cough...

The last file on the bottom had a sticky note stating: had chicken pox.

The name on that file was Khallie Saran.

⨯ 18 ⨯

LEFT IN THE DUST

AFTER THE LAST bell, Sam rushed out of his classroom and grabbed his bike in the rack by the parking lot.

"*Pssst*, Sam, over here."

Sam braked and glanced over his shoulder. "Behind you."

Sam turned around and spotted Blake and his brother in the van that Colton had parked behind a blazing red maple tree. The window was rolled down, and Blake was signalling for him. Sam's bike crunched across the gravel and onto the parking lot.

"How's your cat?" Blake asked.

Sam shrugged his shoulders. "Pix seems fine. What about the other cats?"

"The vet at the shelter gave them a quick check and they were fine too. They were all returned to their owners."

Colton, who was in the driver's seat, leaned over and said, "The vet wished you'd saved one of those ticks, though. Ticks that make cats practically comatose isn't something she'd ever heard of before."

"I just didn't want one to bite me."

"Yeah, I get it," said Blake with a slight shudder. "Certain things, leeches and ticks and anything that burrows and sucks blood aren't something you want to hold in your hand."

"Got that right," agreed Sam. "What... what's wrong?" he said, noticing the uncomfortable expression that both brothers had, making them look a lot more alike.

"Well, Colton went to the police station to report the cats and the weird lab and..."

"They need to talk to Owen or me?" offered Sam. Blake looked antsy. Other kids were coming down the sidewalk. He probably wanted to get going.

Colton scratched his head. "The police basically accused you guys of pulling some stupid prank. I had to do some fast talking so they didn't think you stole the cats yourselves or trespassed on private property." Colton gripped the steering wheel and favoured Sam with a long serious stare. "Which I don't think you did, of course, but..."

"But what?" Sam sputtered. "Something weird is up with Sinistrus Mansion. I thought they'd send out a police boat."

Blake shook his head. "The police say the mansion is built on bedrock. There's no way there could be a basement, that there never was a basement, that you guys were wasting their time and it's a serious misdemeanour, something called..."

"Causing mischief," Colton finished. "Are you sure that..."

Sam heard Ravi and Andy in the background. They were walking fast and calling Blake's name. He saw Blake wince and without even saying anything to his brother, Colton started the engine.

"I'm sure of what I saw," Sam said quickly.

"We'll talk more in astronomy." Blake waved goodbye as Colton pulled away from the curb.

"Blake, wait, dude, how's it going?" Ravi shouted.

"Hey, man, are you coming back to school now?" Andy broke into a run. "We miss you."

Colton braked but kept the van's engine running.

"I've gotta go," Blake called to his friends. "But soon, dudes, soon. We'll get together."

They all waved and grinned.

"And you guys should get Sam to join the rowing team. He's good."

They glanced at Sam, not exactly looking convinced, but they all nodded in agreement.

"Sure."

"If you say so, Blake."

"We could use another man."

"Are you going to be rowing too? We need you to qualify for the provincial summer games."

"Hey, Blake, Sam!" Owen ran over. "How are the cats? Did you find the owners? What did the police say?"

"Whaa..." sputtered Andy staring at Owen. "Get real. Do you even know who you're talking to?"

Sam watched as Blake simply shook his head and shrugged at his friends, almost in slow motion. "Later, guys," he called, and the van pulled away. Owen was left in the dust, staring down at his not too trendy running shoes.

"Freak." Andy shoved Owen. Then Ravi shoulder-punched him as they walked past him. Owen looked up at Sam, turned on his heels, and walked away.

Sam should have said something, done... something.

× × ×

THAT NIGHT, SAM was fixing himself a mozzarella and leftover meatball sandwich in the kitchen.

"Sammy, Sam, come here!" screeched Molly.

"What?" He raced to Molly and Dory's room. He thought it interesting how one half of the room had a tidy bed, books stacked neatly on shelves, and boxes of crayons, pencil crayons, and gel pens placed carefully on top of the dresser. In the other half of the room, the bed was buried under a heap of clothes, open books, their pages bent back, scattered schoolwork, and—Sam blushed—girls' underwear. How did Dory find anything?

"What's up?" he asked Molly, longing to return to the kitchen and bite into the juicy sandwich that he'd just pulled out of the toaster oven. He could smell the spicy meatballs.

Molly rubbed her eyes and yawned. She padded across the floor in her bare feet, tugging a quilt over her pajamas. "Those wicked cat-napper people were calling for Pix again." Molly glared. "But I slammed the window shut and closed the curtains," she said with a nod of her chin. She folded her arms and stamped her foot. "Somebody should arrest them."

Sam raced to the window and yanked open the curtain. He gazed out into the dark night. Charcoal clouds covered the sky, blotting out the stars and any moonlight. A shrill wind whipped up the bluff and rattled the branches in the arbutus tree in their yard, yanking off a bunch of its leaves.

"Are you sure you didn't hear the wind?" Sam asked.

"I'm sure. They have a whistle and they blow it, and Pix wants to go out and play with them."

"I didn't hear any whistle." Sam gazed through the window again, but he couldn't see anyone outside.

"Course not, silly," Molly sounded exasperated. "Only Pix hears the whistle."

"How do you know?" Sam tugged the curtains shut.

"Because he goes crazy," Molly explained. "He jumped on the window sill, knocked down my doll, and started bashing the window with his head, trying to get outside."

Her Raggedy Ann was sprawled on the floor. But Pix was lying on her bed, purring softly. "Good work, detective Molly," Sam said. "I think you foiled those diabolical cat-nappers."

"What's foiled?" Molly scrunched her face.

"I mean, you stopped them and saved Pix." Sam roughed her hair and steered her back to bed. "C'mon, time for sleep."

"Where's Dory?" Molly half-whined. "I'm scared."

"No, you're not," Sam said softly. "You just fended off a gang of cat-nappers. You rock." Molly smiled, although she didn't look convinced.

"Dory will be back practically by the time you close your eyes," he promised.

"Okay, Sammy Sam, but tuck us in." Molly dived onto her bed. Sam lifted the comforter and pulled it tight. Then he folded part of her quilt over Pix, tucking him in as well.

When he turned out the bedroom light, both of them were snoring.

The kitchen door slammed, and Dory rushed inside.

"Where were you?" Sam asked.

"None of your business," she said.

"It's *my* business." Babcia leaned out of her study. "Come and discuss why you are late for curfew, young lady. And why that has also made you rude to your brother."

"I went to the movies with my friend Angel and she went for popcorn near the end of the movie and didn't return. I kept waiting for her to come back." Dory sounded super annoyed. "Then I drove back to her place to find out what happened, but she wasn't home. She dumped me. But you can't ground me for being a concerned person, right?"

Sam took his plate with the tantalizing meatball sandwich, walked past Babcia's study, and said goodnight.

Like Molly's side of the room, Sam's bedroom showed spit and polish. He could bounce a quarter off his tightly tucked blanket. That's how their dad liked things done, with military precision. Dory, on the other hand, had been mostly raised by her mother, and Sam had only visited one of her homes once. He vaguely remembered a lot of beads, incense, and hanging crystals.

Sam took one more longing look at his juicy sandwich and placed it on his bedside table. Then he opened his window and his checkered curtain fluttered in the strong briny sea breeze. He took a deep breath, climbed out, and got on his bike.

If people were trying to steal cats, Sam knew where they were headed.

× 19 ×

AN EERIE
SYNCHRONICITY

SAM CYCLED TO the wharf across from Croaker's Island. The night was dark and windy. Thick clouds shrouded the island, although Sam thought the clouds over Sinistrus Mansion appeared more green than grey. The tide was out and the pungent smell of kelp filled the air. He chained his bike to a pylon under the wharf, just as he caught sight of shadows moving down from a bluff toward the shore. Sam stepped behind the pylon to hide.

Eight people shuffled past him in a stiff woodenly gait as they crossed the sand stealthily and without uttering a single word. Sam caught his breath and gaped at the macabre parade before him. They were all teenagers.

One by one, the young people lined up in single file along the shore, facing Croaker's Island. At the rear of the line, two of them placed a large carrying case on the beach—the case was like the one Colton had given them for transporting the cats. The rest of the teens stood motionless along the shore.

"Meow, meow…" Sam heard scratching inside the case. He crept toward it, staying hidden behind the wharf pylons. His heart pounded inside his rib cage, but he almost laughed in relief and stepped out when he recognized Angel Chan. This had to be some practical joke. At the last moment he caught sight of the frozen, dead gaze on her face—her empty eyes made the hair on the back of his neck prickle. He decided to stay put for the time being.

A mechanical chugging, like pistons falling into place, rose offshore: thug, click, thug, click, and water began boiling in a direct line from Croaker's Island toward the teens. Sea water splashed as a vertical wave formed. But the wave was forming opposite the tidal pull. How could that be?

Sam watched in amazement as a strange metal stepping bridge surfaced from the waves. That's what had scraped the boat hull when he, Blake, and Owen had rowed to the island. Their boat had crossed the ridges of it. Sam scratched his head. He'd never seen such weird technology.

A witchy phosphorescent blue-green beam flashed below the surface of the water, illuminating the flat, smooth metal bridge, which looked like the backs of giant metal tortoises linked in a narrow chain. The shells rose above the water in soft splashes, making a pathway of stepping stones to Croaker's Island. One by one, the teens began moving on top of the water in an eerie synchronicity, shuffling so stiffly that Sam wondered if these were Molly's zombies.

Sam's jaw dropped. Also illuminated in the witchy light was one young person that he knew was most certainly not a zombie.

Khallie Saran!

Sam's head whirled. Kind, sweet, caring Khallie was a cat-stealer? He . . . he couldn't believe it. But the evidence was right in front of his face. Why? He snapped out of his shock and got to work fast.

Sam crept past the slippery rocks and slime under the wharf until he was directly behind the pylon where Angel had placed the carrying case. As the two teens waited for their turn to cross, Sam reached and pulled the case toward him until he could unlock it. Three cats shot out. A grey tabby bit him and a calico scratched him as they made their escape. "You're welcome," Sam muttered under his breath.

Angel and the tall boy beside her seemed oblivious to what was happening right next to them. It was as if they were completely out of it, dazed and focused only on wading up to their knees in the still surf and walking across the water.

Sam slipped two slimy boulders inside the pet case so it was roughly the same weight as before and pushed it back. He'd barely got the cage latched when Angel and the boy reached down in unison and hoisted the case, with Angel in front and the boy behind. They waded into the water and stepped onto the first metal plate.

As soon as they were a third of the way to the island, Sam crept out from the wharf. Deadly currents and breakwater churned around the half-submerged bridge. Sam's heart was pounding just watching them make their way across. When Angel and the boy reached the shore, Sam swallowed twice, and then set out to follow them and find out what they did once they got to the island.

Sam ignored his cartwheeling stomach. He refused to think about what might be waiting on the other side and at Sinistrus Mansion. Sometimes a person could have too much imagination. He had reached the second stepping stone when the bridge submerged completely, the metal foothold sliding out from under him and almost sending him tumbling into the waves.

What if that had happened when he'd been halfway to the island? He'd have surely drowned. As it was, the cold water soaked his shoes and legs up to his knees. Sam breathed deeply until his blood stopped pounding in his ears. He went back underneath the wharf and waited...

× × ×

SAM BEGAN FEELING like tiny rocks were tied to his eyelashes, weighing them shut. Counting starfish to pass the time had been as soporific as counting sheep. He forced his eyes open again, yawning heavily. He'd sat under the wharf, his windbreaker keeping his butt mostly dry, as he drew his damp knees and legs to his chest. Sam was, for once, grateful for the green-and-yellow striped wool sweater he wore under his jacket. Babcia certainly could knit a warm sweater.

He should have worn his watch, but maybe that would have slowed time down even more as he'd probably have checked it every two minutes. He bit his lip to stay awake, tasting the salt from the soft sea spray that coated his face.

A gurgling erupted across the water, and Sam shot up fully alert, almost bumping his head against the wharf. The night had grown deadly dark. Black clouds hung close to the ground, creating an eerie fog. In the distance, Sam could hear the foghorn from the lighthouse up the coast echoing across the bay. Water splashed and made the familiar churning sound.

The strange stepping stones emerged from the water, the eerie blue-green glow lighting the way. As near as he could tell, the lineup was in reverse order, with Angel and the tall boy crossing first and second. Next were several other people Sam thought he recognized: Timothy Wheeler, Dane Parsons—who was in Dory's group of friends—and Nancy Kim. Some of them were high schoolers, and some were from middle school. What could they all have in common besides belonging to a cat-stealing ring?

Then it hit Sam. Every person he recognized, and he was willing to guess the others too, had been the names on the files he'd found stacked on the nurse's desk at school! These people had not been up to date with their immunization shots—they'd all had mumps or chicken pox or measles or whooping cough.

Khallie Saran crossed the bridge last. Sam waited until she was halfway up the bluff before he grabbed his bike and shot out from under the wharf, scurrying across the sand and the rocks. He scrabbled up the bluff, dragging his bike behind him.

✕ 20 ✕

A HOUSE OF CARDS

DIRT AND ROCKS gave way on the bluff, and Sam lost his footing and fell back into a tangle of brambles. His bike slid halfway down the bluff, catching on a big boulder, where it fell sideways, its wheels spinning. Sam carefully pulled himself from the brambles, but one vine ripped a thin line in his jeans. Babcia would not be impressed; she said she'd never seen anyone so hard on clothes as Sam.

Sam scrabbled down to his bike, which, thankfully, didn't show any bend in the wheel spokes. He started over, dragging his bike to the top of the bluff. The sky had lightened as the clouds thinned and a little moonlight poked through. It occurred to Sam that most of the clouds had gathered off the shore and around the island, as if they were purposely shrouding the creepy place.

Sam peered down the coastal road and noted the weird zombie troop of kids had lost its order. The line was straggled now. Most of the teens had scattered, many leaving the road and heading into town. Although as far as Sam could tell, even if they were headed in the same direction, none of them grouped together or talked to each other. They moved fast and purposely, and some even jogged. It was almost as if they didn't even know someone else was right beside them. He shook his head. Odd.

There was only one shadow sticking to the coastal road—Khallie. Khallie half-ran and half-jogged along the road. Sam waited until she was almost out of sight before he leaped on his bike and started riding. His wet jeans chafed his legs as he pedalled.

To Sam's surprise, he saw his friend turn into the run-down trailer park at the side of the coastal road. He pedalled faster before he lost her in the maze of dilapidated trailers. He followed stealthily as Khallie turned left and then right, and then he lost her. Sam got off his bike, crunched over the gravel, and kept moving. When he neared a broken-down trailer that listed to the side, he tripped over a rock garden someone had laid out by the trailer pad and badly stubbed his foot. He accidentally dropped his bike, which smashed against his shin. Sam tripped over the wheel to pick it back up and banged his knee. A few bad words slipped out—not the worst ones, but bad enough. He rubbed his leg.

"What are you doing here?" someone hissed.

Sam didn't jump as high as the maple bush—not quite...
He spun around. Levelling his voice he said, "Khallie, what
are *you* doing here?"

Fury sparked from Khallie's eyes—tired, bloodshot
eyes. "Why are you spying on me—how... how long have
you been following me?" She clenched and unclenched her
fists. Sam thought she might hit him. He took a step back.

"I followed you back from Croaker's Island. You know—
the place you said you've never set foot on, the place where
I found your bracelet?"

"You followed me from there?" Khallie looked down at
her bracelet and pulled at the silver charms. When she
looked back up, a mix of emotions clouded her face. Astonishment for one, confusion, and anger—yeah, Sam thought
that was the main one.

"I followed you after I let go of the cats you and your
friends stole," Sam said evenly. He couldn't take his eyes
off her face—a face that didn't look one bit evil, not even
when she was furious.

Khallie kept shaking her head. "You're crazy, Sam.
And you're mean."

Mean? The low-down, cat-thieving imposter was calling *him* mean? Sam was confused.

A battered ancient Volkswagen Beetle pulled up on the
gravel. Khallie's eyes widened. "Hide," she told Sam. Then

she turned and crossed the gravel parking lot. Sam ducked back behind the maple bushes.

"What are you doing out? Are you crazy? Do you know what time it is?" The young woman shooting rapid-fire questions swung her legs out of the car and stood up. Despite all the weirdness of the night, Sam drew in a sharp breath. She wasn't much older than Dory, but if he thought Khallie looked like a princess, she looked like a queen. Her long black hair swung far past her shoulders. Bracelets tinkled like bell chimes as they slid up and down her wrists. She wore huge hoop earrings that caught in the trailer porch light.

Sam could imagine her dancing in red swirling skirts around a campfire instead of wearing jeans and a tie-dyed T-shirt and driving a Beetle.

The young woman opened the trunk of her car. "Seriously, Khal, do you want to get sent back to foster care or end up in juvie again?"

Foster care? Sam frowned. What about Khallie's uber-strict parents?

Khallie swiped her arm over her face and took a deep breath. "Azina, I was just stargazing."

"It's cloudy," stated Azina. "Try again. You know what our social worker said—you have a nine o'clock curfew. Mrs. Tutti next door told me she saw you come back late Tuesday evening too."

"That was my astronomy class. I almost made curfew, Sis."

Sister? Sam thought Khallie was an only child.

"Khal, I don't have time for your lame excuses," Azina said wearily. She yanked a cardboard box out of her trunk. "You know if I have to stay here and watch over you, I can't work nights. Do you think I like working for snotty rich people, cleaning their businesses instead of going to college full-time?"

"No," Khallie was barely audible. She took the box from her sister without looking her in the eye.

"But this job keeps us going, Khal." Her sister softened her own voice. "Look at the stuff Mrs. Dubois dumped in the charity box—beautiful clothes just your size, and she also put in a necklace that matches that bracelet I brought home for you." Azina dangled a crystal red heart on a long silver chain. "Can you imagine some rich kid not even wanting this?"

"You can keep it, Azina," Khallie said softly. "You should have something nice too."

Sam knew he shouldn't be listening in on their personal conversation, but he couldn't leave without being discovered by Khallie's sister. He had a pretty good idea that would only make things worse.

Azina slipped the necklace over her head. "Thanks, but let's not get sidetracked." Her expression hardened. "So tell me. What are you doing outside, fully dressed in the middle of the night?"

Khallie drew in a ragged breath. "I . . . don't know what happened. I fell asleep on our couch and . . . woke up here when I heard a crash and a loud noise." She looked straight at the maple bush Sam was hiding behind and then quickly looked away. "I *can't* remember *anything* before that, not even leaving the trailer."

Azina placed both hands on Khallie's shoulders. "You've been sleepwalking? Again? I thought me tying the door shut would help."

Khallie lifted her hand and scratched the back of her neck. "Apparently not," she said so softly that Sam had to lean forward just to hear. Then they both went inside the trailer.

Sam thought Khallie sounded completely sincere when she'd told her sister that she'd been sleepwalking. And she'd seemed genuinely astonished when he had accused her of being on Croaker's Island.

Sam thought there might be some truth in what she was saying about sleepwalking. But how could he trust her when everything she told people about her life was an outright lie—not an embellishment, not a fib, but a truckload of whoppers. Sam completely understood what his father meant about people building a house of cards.

Khallie had built an imaginary life in a house of cards, which was crashing down in front of him.

Sam didn't have a clue how to sort through her tales and find the truth, even though it was key to figuring out what was going on that island.

He could think of one expert on truth twisting, though—Dory.

⨯ 21 ⨯

BAD CHARACTER

MAYBE IT WAS the look on his face, but Dory didn't balk when Sam asked her for a ride to school because he needed to talk to her. Sam jumped into the red Fiat as Dory was taking it out of neutral and rolling out of the driveway.

"What's up, brother?" asked Dory. "I don't think it's because of last night. I explained everything to your grandmother, ah, our *babcia*, that coming home late wasn't my fault. Besides, she's got to get used to the fact this isn't the 1980s, or her old country, and I should have the same freedom as other seventeen-year-olds. That's democracy, right?" Dory frowned. "Babcia... wouldn't have called him, would she?"

"Called who?" Sam put his hand on the steering wheel, steadying the convertible. Dory was weaving her car down the bluff a little randomly like she was upset, and the road was narrow enough when she drove straight.

Dory brushed Sam's hand out of the way like he was an annoying moth. "It's nothing to do with me that Dad's coming..."

Sam's heart leaped into his throat—and not because of Dory's hairpin turn onto the highway. "Dad's coming?" Of course, Dory giving Sam a ride to school was more to do with her own diabolical motives than him asking her for a ride.

Sam's stomach squeezed a little. Their father, Captain Jake Novak, did important work. He couldn't just pick up and leave—not without a critical reason.

"I thought you knew, mate." Dory shook her head.

Sam had slept late after being up most of the night. Babcia and Molly had already left when he'd stumbled into the kitchen for breakfast. "Dad's coming?" He hated how his voice squeaked again.

"Something's up, and it's big, brother." Dory chewed her lower lip and quickly added without a hint of an Australian accent, "And it's not about anything I've done... I don't think..."

Maybe Sam was wrong about Dory not wanting to stay with them in Croaker's Cove. She hadn't complained about living here for a while. Not to mention, he was pretty sure her mother hadn't called once.

Sam got a sinking feeling. What if Babcia had come into his room and discovered he'd been out most of the night? Or what if their grandmother had had enough of Molly's frenzies and insisted on their father taking charge? It could have been any of their faults, and in the end, it didn't really matter why their father was coming. Once he arrived, he'd get them and everything else all back into order, which might include boarding school. "When?"

"Soon." Dory swallowed. She whizzed past the turn that led back to the coastal road and the trailer park, reminding Sam about his problem with Khallie.

"I'll... do what I can to find out what's going on," Sam said.

"Knew I could count on you, mate, to smooth things over," Dory said more cheerily. "We've got to have each other's backs."

Where she would stab me if she had to, Sam thought dismally.

"So what did you want to talk to me about?" Dory asked.

Sam steeled himself. Letting Dory in on his problem was a risk. What to say; what to leave out? There was something strange going on in this town, and he needed to get to the bottom of it, even if his father was coming. Maybe especially, because for whatever reason his dad needed to see them, living in a place where teenagers roamed the night in strange zombie brigades, kidnapping cats and crossing strange mechanical bridges to a haunted island, likely wouldn't be reassuring to most parents.

Sam resolved not to mention that part. Instead he told Dory he'd discovered his friend Khallie had lied about pretending to be a rich girl and about where she lived. "She's always talking about having super-strict parents, but she's been a foster kid and lives in a trailer park with her sister who works as some sort of maid or cleaner. She's created this whole make-believe life she sells to us all."

Dory stared out the windshield and steered the car as if she was making her way through an obstacle course instead of cruising down a quiet street. He wasn't even sure she was listening. Maybe she didn't get how this was gnawing at his gut.

Sam drove his point home. "I... don't think I can trust her, and so I don't know if we should even be friends."

"Get over it," was Dory's sage advice.

But Sam really needed to know more about Khallie's trustworthiness. He needed to know if she was lying about not remembering being on Croaker's Island. "I can't."

"Look, some lies aren't bad; they can even be sort of good," Dory said with more than a hint of impatience.

"What do you mean?" They'd turned down the road that led to the middle school. Low-hanging tree branches tapped against the car roof, scattering coloured leaves on the windshield. Dory turned her wipers on and crunched them into leaf confetti.

She slowed the car and hit the brakes, pulling up across the street from the school parking lot. "When Molly came out this morning in an ugly orange dress, a red sweater, and even uglier purple tights, she asked how she looked and I said very nice. I could tell she really wanted to wear that vile outfit."

Sam couldn't help think how Dory never spared him her critical eye or sharp tongue. The bell rang and students began streaming into the building. Dory didn't seem too worried about either of them making it to school on time. Weren't they in enough trouble with Babcia? He grabbed his pack, ready to race up the steps and into class.

Dory grabbed Sam's shoulder when he opened the car door. "So you see, Sam, some lies are to protect people."

Sam shook his head. His dad always said lying was a sign of bad character. But what about Khallie's acts of kindness? Could a person be bad and good? It didn't matter. He really needed someone he could trust. That wasn't Khallie.

"She isn't trying to protect anybody's feelings. She lies to look like someone she isn't." It almost hurt Sam physically to say it.

Dory gave his shoulder the slightest shake. "Don't you get it, Sam? Khallie is *protecting herself.*"

× 22 ×

ALONE IN
THE UNIVERSE

O N TUESDAY EVENING, as soon as Dory parked in the university parking lot, she raced for the observatory, hoping to catch a glimpse of Blake's family. Sam followed, but stopped when Khallie stepped from the shadows between two parked cars.

"Sam, we have to talk." Khallie had a desperate look in her eyes. "You can't keep avoiding me."

He'd been doing a pretty good job so far. As soon as Khallie turned down a hall at school, he'd turn down another hall. In class, if she tried catching his eye, he'd quickly turn to one of Blake's friends and start a conversation. That was easy—all he had to do was bring up Blake or rowing. If she waited outside the class, Sam took his sweet time asking the teacher about the lesson. Teachers lived for that.

But she'd shown up early for astronomy class and now he was cornered. What do you say to a person who's been spewing a pack of lies, even if it sounds like she's had a hard-luck life?

Sam crooked a weak smile and raised his eyebrows. "So you've been to juvie?"

Khallie let out a nervous laugh. "Not exactly." She sucked air between her teeth. "It was more like a holding facility. Apparently habitually running away from foster homes is against the law." Then she muttered, "I suppose you hate me now."

"Not even close." The words shot out of Sam's mouth before they even hit his brain.

"I haven't run away in over a year, not since Azina turned nineteen and could be my guardian," Khallie said in a rush, "and I won't either. I'm sticking with my sister. It's all I ever wanted."

Khallie reached for Sam's hand. His arm tingled up to his elbow.

"Why are you always saying how your parents are super strict and buying you gifts and..."

A look so troubled crossed Khallie's face that Sam wished he could swallow his words back.

"I know that's how my parents would be," Khallie said softly, "if they were here."

Sam didn't ask her where they were.

"I can't get sent back into foster care, Sam. I'm with my sister on a trial basis, and I can't get into any trouble. You've got to help me."

At first Sam thought Khallie was going to ask him to help her keep the lies going. But instead she asked, "Tell me what you saw me doing. How did I get to Croaker's Island? What... what happens when I'm sleepwalking?"

A dog in a parked car began barking like crazy. A car alarm went off. Sam and Khallie spun around, but they couldn't see anyone. Then they noticed a small halo of white hair bob behind a car.

"My goodness, what a lot of bother." Professor Marigold was wrestling with a car door. Sam went over and helped him untangle the strap of his leather satchel caught on the door handle. The car alarm blared.

"I think we're late," said the professor, checking an old-fashioned fob watch that he'd slipped out of his lab coat pocket. "Come along, come along."

Another dog growled and barked as the professor passed by a white minivan. If the window had been open any wider, Sam was sure the dog would have lunged straight for the professor's throat. He and Khallie followed the professor into the observatory as the bleating horns in the parking lot faded.

Blake sat in his usual chair by the telescope. Sam's stomach tightened uncomfortably when he spotted Owen sitting across the room between Betty and Diane.

"My goodness, you have a lot of badges." The woman named Betty gave Owen an admiring nod at his Scout uniform.

"How sweet you are, sitting with us tonight," said Diane. "Won't your friends miss you?" From the smile that dimpled her face, Sam had the uncomfortable feeling she would reach over and pinch Owen's cheek.

"I can hear the lecture better from here, and thank you for letting me join you," Owen said politely. Owen didn't look at Sam, Blake, or Khallie. Instead, he gazed straight at Professor Marigold, who dug through his satchel for his lecture notes.

"What did you two do to Owen?" Khallie's harsh whisper dripped menace. Sam swallowed and saliva stuck in his throat.

"I dunno what Owen's problem is," said Blake.

"What. Did. You. Two. Do?" She repeated icily.

Sam knew Khallie wouldn't let them off the hook. He let out a hiss of breath and started. "You know how Owen doesn't always pick the best time to talk about confidential stuff?" he began. Her eyes seared through him, choking off his excuse.

"I kind of pretended I didn't know Owen when I was in the car with Colton," Blake admitted. "And Andy and Ravi, ah, I guess they…" He couldn't look Khallie in the eye.

"I should have spoken up when Andy and Ravi were being jerks after Blake left," Sam confessed. "They didn't believe Owen was Blake's friend." He didn't look away, but he withered under Khallie's accusatory gaze.

"You know… we're trying to keep our investigation of the ocean echoes secret and…" Sam's heart beat loudly in his chest. Making up excuses was just weak. Khallie, the cat-napper, didn't try and wiggle out with any excuses when he'd called her out about juvie. He mumbled, "I should have stuck up for him."

Khallie stood up and joined Owen and the two ladies. Owen's eyes shone as he said hi.

"To what do we owe this honour?" asked Diane.

"I just wanted to join your *friendly* group," Khallie said lightly as she shot daggers Sam and Blake's way.

That was Khallie—she wasn't afraid to take a stand. Not like him. That got Sam thinking:

Fact: Khallie had never actually lied that she'd been an only child. He'd assumed that because she never mentioned a sibling.

Fact: She also never told people she was a rich girl, even though she had lied about where she'd lived. Or had she?

She'd just let other kids assume she lived in the swanky Oceanview neighbourhood by showing up there for the school bus.

Fact: She had definitely lied about having strict parents. Or had she? She'd said her parents would have been strict. Sam's throat thickened. Khallie must have had a mom and dad who cared about her and watched over her at one point. When Andrea Kellerman had asked her where she'd got her charm bracelet, she hadn't specifically told her it was from her parents—only that they gave her gifts.

That didn't change the final fact: Khallie had deliberately misled people into thinking that she was someone different. She had created the perfect cover with strict parents, so no one ever gossiped about her not bringing friends over to her place, or why she couldn't go out with them when she was under curfew.

Sam suddenly understood what Dory meant about the things people did to protect themselves. Khallie hid behind imaginary parents to keep her safe. Blake, basically a nice guy, would deny his interest in nerd stuff. He'd even ignore a friend, all so he could maintain his reputation as a cool jock.

As for Sam, if he was going to be honest, he hid behind hesitation. Like when he competed in a race or had to step up to the plate to help a friend, he'd freeze rather than take ownership or risk failing.

Didn't he also make things up about his mother, like she still sometimes guided him? Like now, when he could almost hear her voice saying, *Trust the girl, Sammy. She's telling the truth about her sleepwalking.*

None of them was perfect. Owen was the only one of all of them who was comfortable in his own skin. That's why he couldn't care less if people overheard him talking about slow motion or bloop echoes, or any science stuff, or all his skills from Scouts.

The three of them needed each other if they were going to get to the bottom of the strange underwater noises, the cat-nappers, zombie-like teens, and that weird laboratory hidden beneath Sinistrus Mansion.

"Once more, Master Owen, I'll explain to you why there can't be any outer-space visitors landing on planet Earth. We are alone in the universe." Professor Marigold let out an exasperated sigh.

Sam snapped to attention and tried to remember what Owen had said moments before. It had been important.

"What an odd astronomy class this has been," Betty said to her friend. "All we ever do is argue if there can be other life in the universe. I thought we'd be gazing at Saturn's rings."

✕ 23 ✕

WE DO HAVE
A PROBLEM

PROFESSOR MARIGOLD stood on his tiptoes, leaned over his lectern, and rustled the pages of notes he hadn't touched. Warm air hissed through the heating vents in the observatory, and because he hadn't opened the dome for the giant telescope yet, it was getting uncomfortably hot. Sam's back prickled with sweat under Babcia's newest brown-and-orange checkered sweater.

"What we *do* know, Master Owen, is that only a small fraction of stars have planets, and only a tiny fraction of those planets are exo-planets, and only a teeny-tiny, teensy-weensy fraction of exo-planets might be in the Goldilocks Zone—neither too cold nor too hot so they can have life-giving oceans. Only a minute, minuscule, micro-fraction of those planets might actually have water and develop any sort of life, and only a mini-minute, micro, teeny-tiny..."

"We get it. You mean it's possible no other planets have life on them," Blake broke in.

"Yes, well," Professor Marigold adjusted his lab coat. "As I was saying, it is therefore completely unlikely any other planets might develop *intelligent* life."

"Only unlikely? So, Earth *isn't* the only planet with life," Owen said, as if the professor was agreeing with him, which Sam was pretty sure he wasn't.

"Fine," Professor Marigold said in a way that reminded Sam of Babcia when she meant anything *but* fine. "Think about this. If there *is* intelligent life, there are a lot older stars and planets than Earth in the universe, which would then mean they'd have a very advanced civilization. But what have we heard from them?"

Sam, Blake, and Khallie shrugged.

"Zippo, zero, not a peep." The professor nodded in a self-satisfied way.

"What's an exo-planet?" asked Diane.

"A planet that isn't made of gas," explained Owen.

"Not Saturn's rings," said Betty rather wistfully.

Sam shot up his hand. "Maybe we don't have the right technology to hear them yet, Professor, sir." Molly's favourite storybook was *Horton Hears a Who*. She'd ask Sam to read it to her regularly. In that story, Whos were shouting, but Horton couldn't hear them until it was almost too late.

"We've only being transmitting radio signals since the 1920s," Sam explained. "Maybe we just haven't been searching long enough."

"You'd also need broader bandwidths to detect signals across great distances," said Owen. "Right, Professor Marigold?"

Professor Marigold ignored Owen, so Owen continued to make his point. "Professor, I read a theory that maybe aliens don't *want* to contact us directly. Did you take that into account? Like I was saying *before*, outer-space visitors could check us out using nanotechnology—tiny machines we can't even see." Owen raised his voice. "Nanobots could be all around us and we wouldn't even know it."

"No, no... no," the professor muttered. "This isn't Disneyland or a make-believe *Star Wars* movie. Forget this nonsense. Don't lose your tempers in a teapot."

"You mean 'make a tempest in a teapot.'" Sam hoped his face remained calm even though his heart was racing and his head was buzzing. *No way*, he argued with himself. The rest of astronomy class floated by Sam as he tried to get his thoughts organized.

Sam barely heard the ladies politely request that they start gazing at planets and could they please see Saturn's rings. He sort of remembered that when the professor obliged them and dilated the observatory roof to raise the telescope, he caught a chill when cold air whooshed in and collided with his sweaty neck. He did recall the ladies muttering how they weren't getting their money's worth that evening because for some reason the professor dismissed the class twenty minutes early.

Mostly, Sam couldn't wait for class to be over and for the professor and the ladies to leave. "Khallie, Owen, please don't leave. I really need to talk to you," Sam said when they stood up. Owen rolled his eyes.

"Khallie, I... there's stuff you should know," Sam pleaded.

"My parents will be here soon." Blake dropped the hint that they should clear out.

Sam turned to Blake. "There are things you and Owen should know too, important things. I... think Croaker's Cove is in terrible danger."

Sam turned back and faced Owen, but he levelled his gaze at Khallie. "Good friends should forgive each other, right, Khallie? Owen, I'm really sorry I didn't stick up for you in front of Andy and Ravi. I... I was trying to stay under their radar myself, but I won't do that again."

Owen hung his head. "I guess I know now it's better to stay under the radar sometimes."

Khallie walked over and elbowed Blake. "Say it."

Blake sighed. "I was a jerk. But I don't want rumours going around about me. You've got to keep things quiet and not blab..." Khallie elbowed him again. "Sorry. No excuse." Blake held out his hand. Owen took it and they shook.

"What else was it you wanted to tell us?" Khallie asked Sam. She sounded nervous, like she was worried how much Sam planned to tell people about her. Sam stuck to what his father called pertinent facts. Sam explained how the cats had been in a strange sleep when he'd found them on the island.

"Yeah, it was ticks, right?" Blake checked the time on the round clock on the observatory wall. "Go on."

"Well," Sam shrugged, "the scratches on the back of their shaved necks looked exactly like what I've seen on your neck, Khallie. I believe somebody put them there."

"I've got a tick?" Khallie's hand shot to her neck.

"What? That's not good." Blake paled.

"I could try and burn it out with a match," volunteered Owen. "I've got my first-aid badge."

"No." Khallie's eyes widened, but she turned and lifted up her long black hair, exposing her neck. The scratches still looked red and angry. Gingerly, Sam pointed to a small bump, like a giant pimple on the back of Khallie's neck.

Unlike with Pix, there was no tick exposed, but when his fingers grazed her skin, the swelling squirmed.

"Ugh. Get it out of me!" snapped Khallie.

Blake's eyes popped when he saw the pimple move. Owen let out a low whistle.

"Khallie." Sam took a deep breath and plunged ahead. "I... I think one of those tiny technology thingies, those nanobots, is buried under your skin. What I found in the cats' scratches weren't ticks. I think they're... nanobots and they take control of you. You steal cats and you walk across a submerged mechanical bridge and take them to Croaker's Island."

Khallie spun around. "Don't play me, Sam." Her voice shook with fury.

"Khallie's the cat-napper?" Blake and Owen said in unison. Then they both shook their heads and like doppelganger echoes said, "No way."

"Think hard about this. Some part of you *must* know that I'm telling you the truth." Then it hit Sam. "Think about those bad dreams you've been having. I bet they're the same nightmares Angel Chan has about walking across water to Croaker's Island and seeing ghostly white owls."

When Sam mentioned the owls, he gave Owen a pointed look. Owen scratched his head and looked thoughtful.

"Those aren't dreams when you lose track of time. That's what happens when you sleepwalk." Sam turned to Blake. "It was the underwater bridge we scraped the boat on."

Blake's eyes widened. "That would be super-advanced technology. Colton and I tried to measure the depth off the island once on sonar, but it's too deep to measure. Who could make a bridge like that? Do you think it might have to do with those *slowdown* echoes we've recorded on the spectrogram?"

"Like some kind of underwater secret weapon," Sam said, allowing himself to sound a little satisfied that he'd called it.

"I saw those ghostly, blurry owls too. So did Sam. That wasn't a dream, so maybe the rest..." Owen frowned, shrugged, and said, "could also be true."

For a moment Khallie stared at Sam. Then her eyes brimmed with tears. "Sam, what's happening to me?"

"It's not just you. It's Angel Chan and others. It's like..." He pounded his fists together in an ah-ha moment. "It's all the kids who had files on the nurse's desk, kids who hadn't had immunization shots but had childhood diseases like measles and chicken pox. Someone is using that nanotechnology you were talking about, Owen, some little teeny transmitter to collect data on cats and teenagers."

"Or using cats as spies?" suggested Owen. "There's a whole conspiracy theory about that."

"Why not dogs?" Khallie asked. Everybody stared at her. She shrugged. "Just curious."

"Dogs bark too loud at strangers. No one notices cats creeping around. And those echoes—they're from SUOs," a voice said from behind.

They spun around. Sam's heart took a dive when he spotted Dory standing behind them. "Huh?" He said.

"Submerged Unidentified Objects," said Dory. "It is common knowledge in Australia, mates, that flying saucers hide in underwater caves in our deepest ocean trenches so we don't know aliens are visiting us from other planets."

"Common knowledge?" Sam raised his eyebrows doubtfully.

"Something very mysterious *is* going on." Blake rubbed his legs. "I hate to say it, but I think Dory's onto something."

Dory nodded. "Of course I am."

"That's why we recorded those loud echoes, the *slowdowns*," Owen said slowly. "I've heard about that conspiracy theory too, that large submerged flying objects cause mysterious underwater echoes. And if that's true, I bet someone is messing with the audio signals at the Ocean Institute so the authorities don't detect them."

"We... we'd better keep this on the down-low until we do some more investigating," Blake said nervously. "I mean, people will think we're crazy."

"Too late," said Dory. "I've already texted George, the guy with the podcast *Unexplained Phenomena*."

Sam finally noticed that Dory had her cellphone out and had been tapping it the whole time they were talking.

"My, then, children, we do have a problem, don't we?" said Professor Marigold.

✕ 24 ✕

THE TICKING
CLOCK

THE PECULIAR LITTLE professor skulking in the shadows had taken on a more menacing appearance. Sam watched as Dory opened and closed her hand holding the cellphone. She stared at it as if she could will it away. Blake furtively glanced at the ticking clock on the observatory wall as if he wished his parents would show up that second. Khallie and Owen took half a step back.

It's funny the stuff you notice when you've been stabbed with sudden fear, Sam thought slowly. The giant telescope took on a lurking presence under the dim lighting in the observatory. *And it's hard to get your brain working.* All Sam could think was, *We're in danger.* That pounding shout in his head was so distracting his eyes had black spots dancing in front of him.

Standing close beside Professor Marigold, Sam remembered the uncanny sensation he experienced whenever they crossed paths, as if an icy breeze had shot past him. He recalled when he'd spotted the little man dropping a triangular object off a bluff...

You know what that was, said the soft voice inside him. A hydrophone—an underwater recorder!

Building after building on the campus began shutting down the lights, and it was growing very dark outside as everyone went home. The deserted college became as still as a glassy sea, the only sound the hissing of air through the heating vent. A memory resurfaced, and Sam recalled an incident after his first astronomy class.

"You... you went into the empty building of the Ocean Institute after it was dark. You disconnected the feed from the hydrophones so no one could see the slowdown echoes."

Professor Marigold held out his hands and gave the slightest shrug. "Sorry, friends, but I must nip this in the flower."

"The bud," Sam automatically answered.

"Why didn't you want the Institute seeing the slow-down echoes, Professor Marigold?" asked Owen.

"Were you just... are you threatening me?" asked Dory. Sam and the others huddled closer.

Blake stretched himself higher in his chair and fixed the professor with a fierce expression. "There's five of us and only one of you."

"And, if you'll, um, excuse me, Professor, but you're not..." Sam didn't want to say anything rude by bringing up Professor Marigold's tiny stature. "You should let us leave peacefully, sir," he said firmly.

"Oh, it isn't me you need worry about," said the little man. Did his ears just wiggle? "When that message the young lady sent becomes part of the podcast episode, it will alert a group that you *don't* want knowing what you've been up to." His odd squeaky voice had taken on an ominous shrillness. "In a short time, they will dispatch a message to move the mission to an urgent level. That will bring reinforcements—something you don't want."

"Told you this had to do with SUOs," Dory couldn't help adding.

"Or a government conspiracy to control cats and people with mechanical ticks," said Sam, remembering the zombie parade of teens doing *somebody's* bidding.

"Yes," the professor said noncommittally. "And that puts you all in, what is it you call it, a cucumber?"

"A pickle," corrected Sam.

"Are you with them or against them, that group who will put us in danger?" asked Blake.

Again the professor put up his hands and shrugged.

"What's going on in Sinistrus Mansion?" demanded Sam. "What's lurking below Croaker's Island?"

Professor Marigold cleared his throat. "Let me see if I correctly heard your conversation. You have spotted blurry white owls on the island, and you have seen an underwater bridge. Cats have been disappearing, and teenagers who have had common childhood diseases are being summoned to the island."

All of them nodded.

"Sounds very low-tech," the professor muttered.

"Pardon?" asked Sam.

"The aliens are not from a very advanced civilization." Professor Marigold placed his hand over his mouth. "Perhaps I shouldn't have said that."

"Too late now," said Sam, although he was pretty sure the professor had meant to say exactly that. He was starting to get dots in front of his eyes again. "You're saying Croaker's Cove is being invaded by aliens?"

The others went dead quiet. Even Dory seemed dumbfounded to have one of her crazy theories affirmed.

Professor Marigold took off his thick eye-glasses and rubbed them against his lab coat. Placing the wire spectacles back on his nose, he peered at Sam and his friends. "You seem like nice kids," he said. "A little snoopy, maybe, and a few of you might be too smart for your own good, but nice. I only wish I could help."

Then the little man turned and began walking away.

"Wait!" Sam shouted. "You can't tell us we're under invasion, and kids and cats are being experimented on, and then walk away."

The professor halted and slowly turned around. "I'm sorry, but I'm under strict orders not to get involved."

"But what will happen to us?" pleaded Khallie. "What's going to happen to me?"

"I could try and dig the nanobot out with my Scout knife," offered Owen.

"Harsh," said Blake.

"I wouldn't recommend that," the professor said, shaking his head. "The teeny robot will automatically bury itself deeper, no matter how hard you dig in your knife."

"Eew," Dory grimaced.

"Maybe I should burn it out, like it really was a tick," said Owen, digging through his uniform pockets for matches.

"There will be no knives, no digging, and no burning." Khallie put her hands on her hips.

"An electromagnet would deactivate it." Professor Marigold hesitated, as if he was trying to make up his mind about what to say next. "You're up against a COS."

Looking at their blank faces, the professor explained, "That's a Class One Society. Any Class One Society is not a particularly advanced civilization. They can't appear in their physical form, for example; they need to implant those tiny nanobots you thought were ticks and take minor control of people's minds to get them to do their bidding. Very primitive, you see." The professor muttered again, "They can't even hijack brains; they have to put their subjects in a sleepwalking trance. That's practically a Stone Age civilization."

"If a civilization can travel here from a distant galaxy and build laboratories and bridges under our ocean," Sam started pacing, "and then turn people into sleepwalking zombies so they can run a few tests on humans, they're still *way* ahead of us."

"What would that make our civilization?" asked Owen. "Class Zero?"

"Not quite," said the professor. "But the important point is that these... beings... aren't *that* far ahead of you. That's why they're hiding beneath the sea. They're trying to determine what germs and diseases they'll be exposed to once they take the next step."

"The next step?" Blake gripped the arms of his chair. "That doesn't sound good."

Sam paused for a second. "Wait a minute. That's why the school nurse kept bugging me for my immunization records."

"I... I remember the nurse calling me to her office," Khallie said breathlessly. "She'd received a small patch that was supposed to go behind my neck for one day because I hadn't had some shots." Khallie shook her head. "Right after I took the bandage off, I got what I thought were mosquito bites."

"Does that mean these... aliens... can also monitor our Internet and computers and send messages out to people like the nurse without our knowledge?" Sam tried not to let his voice squeak.

Blake pounded his fists this time. "That's diabolical."

"And pretty smart," Owen said with a touch of admiration.

"I knew it was aliens," said Dory.

"Why make it all the way to Earth and try to get control of a few teenagers and cats?" asked Sam. "If they're more than advanced than us, why would they even care?"

"It's funny," Professor Marigold said softly. "People here are always hunting for rare minerals or gold or diamonds, or oil, yet they sell off or carelessly pollute the most valuable resource in the entire universe."

"What?" asked Blake and Dory.

Sam thought he knew, though Owen said it first. "Water?"

"Precisely," said Professor Marigold.

"We have to stop them, Professor!" Khallie looked fierce and went into lecture mode. "You can't just tell us about aliens who are up to no good and then abandon us."

"But you *aren't* abandoning us, are you?" said Sam.

The professor turned around and began walking away.

✕ 25 ✕

GAMMA RAYS,
I THINK

HERE WAS a weird static in the air, constantly buzzing and making Sam think time had stopped. But when he looked at the clock, it surprised him to see its hands ticking along. Blake's parents were late, Khallie had missed her bus, and any moment now Owen's parents would come looking for him. Professor Marigold stopped halfway out the observatory room with his back to Sam and his friends. If he really wanted to abandon them, then why was he still there?

Sam cleared his throat. "Professor Marigold, when Dory texted George, you said *we* had a problem. I'm thinking you meant you did too."

When the professor didn't turn around, Blake gave it a shot. "You've been tracking those ocean echoes yourself, spying on those… aliens. Don't try and tell us you don't care."

"I don't think you meant it when you said you can't get involved," said Sam.

"Oh, I very much meant it," the professor said so quietly Sam had to step closer to hear. "It's simply not permitted."

Sam tried to ignore how the hair prickled against the back of his neck when he stood so closely to the professor, and he remembered again the dogs barking in the parking lot when the professor walked past them.

"Okay, perhaps you can't get involved yourself, but I think you *want* to help us. You don't want those aliens messing with us." Sam waited.

The professor's shoulders stooped slightly. "You are very intuitive, Sam." Then he focused his gaze on Owen. "And, Master Owen, you're a very clever fellow."

Owen beamed a smile then remembered their dire situation and looked serious again.

Professor Marigold reached into his enormous lab coat pocket and pulled out a pen and paper. Hastily he scribbled something, crumpled up the paper, and tossed it on the floor. "As I said, those beings submerged in your ocean know they are not very advanced, and that there are... other civilizations far, far ahead of them."

The professor raised his voice and emphasized every word. "If... for some reason... they thought one of those *other*... civilizations... found out about their little hijinks, they'd vamoose. They'd blow the soda stand."

"They'd what?" asked Blake.

"Blow this pop stand. Get out fast," answered Sam, rushing to pick up the crumpled paper.

Then the professor scurried away.

Khallie stared at his back as he disappeared into the shadows. "Why do you suppose he kept telling us in astronomy class that Earth is probably the only place in the universe that has intelligent life and..." she gingerly scratched the back of her neck, "now he tells us we've got aliens?"

"My grandmother has a saying for that," Sam said thoughtfully. "Pulling the wool over our eyes."

"Like a smoke screen," added Blake.

"Or camouflage," Owen said nodding. "Not that Professor Marigold blends in much."

"Do you mean..." Dory let out a sharp breath. "You don't suppose your professor is an... an..." She blinked several times. "No way."

Sam unfolded the paper and stared at a diagram dotted with numbers. He had no idea what it meant.

Seeing his blank face, Blake looked over Sam's shoulder. "I've got nothing. Owen, take a look here. The professor must have been dropping a hint when he said you were smart, right?"

"I thought he was just complimenting me," said Owen.

"What about me? Why not let me see if I understand it?" complained Khallie. She glanced at the scribbling. "Never mind."

"Just give the paper to the brainiac," snapped Dory. "We don't have a lot of time."

Sam handed Owen the paper. "Well?"

Owen scrunched his face as he examined the diagram. He muttered numbers under his breath. For a few moments he stared until a nervous tick twitched above his eye. Just as Sam started worrying that the professor had overestimated his intelligence, Owen said, "It... it's a radio broadcast, but on a wavelength I've never seen before. It's a very broad band meant for gamma rays, I think."

"Hey, wait a minute." Sam slowly smiled. "Professor Marigold said those aliens would get out of here fast if they thought someone more advanced had found out about them coming here. I bet if we broadcast that signal, those aliens will think they're in big trouble." He frowned. "Um, can we broadcast it? Will you be able to transmit it?"

Owen nodded. "I think so, but because it's such a weird wavelength, I'd have to set up the receiver really close to that alien ship."

"You mean go back to Croaker's Island?" Ice water trickled through Sam's veins.

"Yeah, and I don't have time to waterproof the receiver. So we'd have to set up the receiver in that basement laboratory we stumbled across." Owen looked at Sam. "Sorry, I can't be the one to do that. I have to transmit from somewhere close by. Besides, my allergies would go nuts and the sneezing would set off the alarm again."

"For crying out loud, why doesn't the professor hand this over to the military or any authority?" said Khallie. "Why us?"

Owen waved his hand dismissively as he studied the paper. "There isn't time for red tape. Besides, if he wants to stay under the radar, no one listens or pays attention to kids."

The ice water was now gushing through Sam's veins. "I guess I'll be going back into the mad scientist laboratory." Then Sam remembered, "But the boat has a hole in it from our last trip. How will we get on the island?"

"I can get the keys to the yacht club." With a sly smile Blake added, "My dad just got a new sailboat. We can it take out and cross over to the island. I... don't know much about sailing, but the boat has a motor."

Sam thought Blake looked a little nervous. "Are you sure?"

"I sailed with Colton... once." With more resolve, Blake declared, "I can manage it. Meet me at my place as soon as you can."

"You girls should stay home." Sam gulped. "Especially if something happens to us, you need to get the word out."

"Not likely." Khallie fastened Sam with a glare. "Those aliens messed with me. That makes it personal. I'm going with you."

"And I'm in too." Dory noticed Sam's frown. With that twisted smile of hers she said, "After all, I'm your expert on aliens."

Sam was getting a bad feeling about this plan.

"Blake, we're so sorry." Mrs. and Mr. Evans rushed into the observatory, with Mr. Evans pushing the wheelchair. "Every traffic light was red," said Mrs. Evans.

"Then we couldn't get through the electronic gate to the parking lot," Mr. Evans said in an annoyed voice. "I had to walk around campus until I found a custodian with a key."

Mr. Chatterjee followed behind them. "Owen, let's get going. Hey, where's your Scout troop?"

"One hour," Blake mouthed to Sam, Dory, Owen, and Khallie.

× 26 ×

SOMETHING'S WRONG
WITH KHALLIE

WHEN SAM AND DORY snuck away from their house, Dory kept the car in neutral as they coasted down the bluff to the road. "So let me get this straight. Suddenly, it's okay with you if I drive passengers that are not family members, even if I only have a novice driver's licence? I thought you were going to rat me out to Dad when he got here."

"You're going to start obeying rules when our town and maybe our planet are at stake?" asked Sam. But Dory didn't answer.

"Okay, I promise I won't mention you driving friends around when Dad gets here," said Sam. "We need your help tonight."

"Whatever." Dory turned the engine on and they shot down the coastal road toward the trailer park. Sam wished this scheme didn't include Dory, but her ability to drive was handy. He realized any power he had over her was now pretty much gone.

Sam stared out the windshield. A patch of moonlight broke through the clouds, lighting the ocean and giving it an unearthly turquoise glow. Sam stared at its briny depths, thinking about the sinister threat hiding beneath those waves. Dory took a sharp left, almost knocking Sam out of his seat. They turned into the trailer park and waited.

When Khallie appeared beside the car, she had to call softly before Sam even saw her. She was practically invisible. She'd dressed for spy work in black jeans, black boots, and a black hoodie. She'd slung a leather messenger bag over her shoulder.

Dory glanced at the dilapidated trailers and Khallie's clothes, but all she said was, "Nice outfit and coordinating designer bag."

"Thanks." Khallie shrugged. "Do we go get Owen now?"

Sam climbed into the back seat, trying to adjust his too-long sweater and tamp down his wild hair as Khallie rattled directions. They started rolling.

Owen stood on the outskirts of his yard, hiding behind the large oak tree that blocked his parents' view from the front window. He shouldered a bulging backpack that almost toppled him backwards when he slid into the back seat of Dory's red Fiat.

"Whoa!" Sam reached out and steadied the heavy backpack. "What have you got in there?"

"Lots of stuff," said Owen. "A Scout is always prepared." The tiny fold-out seats in the back of the Fiat Spider didn't have much room for giant backpacks. Sam and Owen were stuffed in like sardines.

As they approached Blake's place, they saw the house was dark. Dory cut the engine and parked a little way down the street. Blake sat in his wheelchair in the shadows of the driveway. Sam got out of the car first.

Blake hesitated before he said, "Sam, you can come with me, if that's okay. Everyone else meet us at the yacht club down the hill."

"No problem," said Sam. Khallie waved out the window and gave Blake the thumbs-up.

Blake wore racing gloves and wheeled himself for several blocks. Sam jogged beside him just to keep up. But when they got to the top of the hill that led down to the water and the yacht club, Sam got behind the wheelchair and made sure Blake didn't roll down too fast. That is, until…

"Oh, no!" Sam's voice squeaked, and he forced it lower. "That's Angel Chan."

"Why is she walking so weird?" Blake leaned forward from his chair, peering down to the seawall. "Isn't that Dane? And look, turning the corner, it's Nancy Kim." He rubbed his eyes. "Why are they so stiff... like robots?"

"They must be under the command of those nanobots in their necks," decided Sam. "When they're activated, it's like they're sleepwalking."

They turned to each other. "Khallie!"

"Jump on the back of my chair and hang on tight," said Blake. "And give us a hard push."

"Are you sure?"

"Do it. We've got to hurry." Blake leaned forward in his chair and gripped the arms. Sam took a deep breath, gave the chair a push, and then jumped on the back. The wheelchair flew down the hill as scrub and brambles and dust flew past them.

"Lean left!" shouted Blake.

Sam shifted his weight and the chair nudged far enough left to miss a rock. They raced to the bottom of the hill, and Sam leaned his weight far right, bringing the chair up on one wheel as they tore around the corner and into the yacht club beside the wharf gate.

Blake laughed wildly. "Sam, we've got to sign up for bobsledding this winter. That was one awesome ride."

Sam grinned until he remembered that staying in Croaker's Cove depended on a lot of things: right at the top of the list was saving this town from a giant SUO.

Owen burst around the corner and ran toward them. "Something's seriously wrong with..." Owen bent over gasping for air. He pulled out his inhaler and took a deep breath. "...Khallie."

Sam and Blake raced toward the parking lot.

$\times$ **27** $\times$

I'M NO PRINCESS

KHALLIE SAT IN the shotgun seat of the Fiat Spider. Her arms and legs were flailing. Dory was sitting on top of her.

"She went berserk," Dory told Sam while she struggled with Khallie. "I had to cram her in the car, but... Ow! Khallie, don't kick! What's wrong with you?"

"It's the nanochip in her neck," Sam said. "It's been activated."

"We just spotted Angel, Dane, and Nancy doing a weird zombie walk toward the water," explained Blake.

"What are we going to do?" Sam despaired.

"Something soon, I hope. Ow," complained Dory.

Owen huddled over his backpack, fidgeting with wires. Then he raced toward the car. "Quick, move the hair off Khallie's neck."

"Why?" Sam narrowed his eyes, spread himself in front of the car door, and didn't let Owen get any closer. Khallie had been clear she didn't want Owen digging out the chip with his Scout knife or melting it down with matches.

"Professor Marigold said an electromagnet might deactivate the chip," Owen said with a slight wheeze. "So, I brought one. Ah, it should be painless."

"Let the brainiac get to work," grouched Dory. "My legs are going purple with bruises."

Sam climbed into the back seat, grabbed Khallie's shoulders, and held on tight. Owen gingerly untangled her hair and pushed her head forward. She snapped it back.

"For crying out loud, she's not made of glass," said Dory. She twisted around and, using both her hands, held Khallie's head still.

Owen held the electromagnet against Khallie's neck with one hand, then connected its wire to the battery he held with his other hand. There was a small spark, a snap, and a whiff of sulphur.

Khallie stopped struggling. A few moments passed, then Khallie said tersely, "Get off me."

"My pleasure," said Dory. Sam released Khallie's shoulders.

"What happened?" Khallie shot out of the car and smoothed her hoodie. She looked at their uncomfortable expressions.

"You were sleepwalking, that's all," said Sam. "But Owen deactivated the nanobot in your neck."

"You drooled a little," Dory added unhelpfully.

"And..." began Owen.

"Never mind! I get it." She hesitated, and then said, "Wait. This is a good thing. This is how we can get on the island and not be detected if there are spy cameras. I can cross the bridge and get into the house with the others and set up the receiver. I'm *supposed* to be with them."

"No way," said Sam. "I can't put you in danger. *I'm* supposed to rescue us."

Khallie shook her head and looked at Sam meaningfully. "You know I'm no princess, so I don't *need* rescuing. I can take care of myself."

"The girl's got that right," said Dory, rubbing her bruised arm.

"We can take the boat around the island to the other side and wait for you there," offered Blake. "It's closer to Sinistrus Mansion, so you can make a quick getaway."

Owen dug in his pack and pulled out the radio equipment. "The receiver's set up... mostly. You need to wind the red wire around one of the metal poles in that weird basement and then attach the black wire to this tiny receiver. Switch the toggle to 'on.' The red light should flash. I'll be able to tell when the receiver's activated and send the message the professor gave me. When it's sent, the light should flash green."

"How is this message thing supposed to work again?" asked Blake.

"If the professor's right," Owen blinked his owlish eyes, "the aliens will think they're under attack. Then we clear out, and I mean really fast. Once those aliens think someone bigger and badder is after them, I've got a feeling we don't want to be anywhere near the underwater caves."

"Ooo-kaaay. Got it," said Khallie.

"Don't these messages have to travel, like, millions of years?" asked Blake.

"Uh-huh," Owen said matter-of-factly. "This transmission is meant to make the aliens *only think* they're getting a final warning from an advanced civilization of space cops."

There was something about the plan Sam didn't like. Well, there were lots of things he didn't like, but one worry niggled at him. He just couldn't put his finger on exactly which one.

Instead, he said, "Those metal stones are slippery, Khallie. What if you fall off into the sea?" *Don't do this*, he wanted to say but didn't.

"I won't slip." Khallie placed the receiver in her messenger bag and set out. "I've got to hurry and join the others." Before Sam could protest further she shot away, and in the next moment she'd joined Timothy

Wheeler, who was down the road doing his step-stomp zombie stagger.

Blake took out his key and unlocked the gate to the yacht club wharf. The door swung open and he began wheeling toward a sailboat with the name *Peaceful Dream* painted on its hull. Owen and Dory followed him.

"We need to get to the island fast," Sam said through his teeth. "And I'm not waiting in the boat. I'm going to meet up with Khallie at the mansion."

Sam didn't like this plan. He didn't like it at all.

× 28 ×

SOMEBODY SCREAMED

"IT WAS BETTER when we thought the echoes were giant sea monsters lurking below us," Blake said.

Sam couldn't argue with that. Blake steered the sailboat around to the other side of the island. Beyond the shore was open sea, and the horizon opened its inky darkness above, darkening the water below. A seal barked apprehensively somewhere in the restless waves.

Sam eased back the throttle on the gas. "Whoa! We've already emptied most of the tank."

"We're going too fast then," said Blake, who was at the steering wheel. "Take it down to one knot."

"No way. We've got to get to Khallie," insisted Sam.

"I can actually sail if we have to," said Owen. "I've got my sailing badge."

Dory gazed at the merit badges completely covering Owen's Scout uniform. "Of course you do." She put her head down on her knees. "Is anyone else getting seasick?" she muttered.

"There." Sam pointed to the old boat dock. "That's where we can tie up."

"That wharf's a piece of junk," said Blake, looking at the missing planks and the tilting pylons.

"It'll be fine," said Sam.

Blake steered *Peaceful Dream* as Owen and Sam threw out the buoys, buffering the sailboat's hull against the dock. Sam jumped onto the wobbly wharf and tied the rope to a teetering post. The dock groaned menacingly. It shook and groaned even more as Dory leaped onto the wharf.

"What are you doing?" asked Sam.

"Coming with you," said Dory. "Remember, *I'm* the alien expert." The wharf lurched and she clutched her stomach.

His sister looked green enough to *be* an alien.

"Owen, hand me your bag of tricks," said Sam.

"What are you looking for?" Owen looked reluctant to part with his pack.

"In case we need another wire or something," said Sam.

Owen sighed and passed it over. "Careful. There's valuable stuff inside."

Sam shouldered the pack. Then he and Dory headed toward Sinistrus Mansion.

"Don't get close enough to set off any alarms!" shouted Blake. Then he clapped his hand over his mouth, probably realizing shouting was not a good idea when they were trying to sneak around.

Sam and Dory scrambled up the scrub-shot bluff, past raw and wounded-looking arbutus trees, and out to where the island levelled off. Along the trail, dry needles crunched under their feet and gave off a sharp pine scent. Sam broke through the last scattering of trees and then halted.

"Hmmph." Dory bumped into him from behind.

Sam pointed at four of the zombie troop stumbling down the stairs and moving with surprising speed back to the bridge. They were the younger kids, not the high schoolers.

"What's up with them?" said Dory.

Nothing good, Sam figured. They hid behind a gnarled and twisted arbutus tree beside Sinistrus Mansion as the other kids passed by.

"This place seriously creeps me out," said Dory.

Sam realized they were underneath the branches where he'd seen the ghostly owls.

"Eew, eew, get it off, get it off!" Dory cried out. She tore at thick cobwebs hanging off the tree branches.

When Sam reached for her, he got tangled in the webs and began yanking a few sticky strands from his own skin, but the cobweb only stretched. Tacky white threads clung to his face. More piles of webbing slipped off the branches, falling onto Dory.

"I can't get it off!" Dory strangled back a scream. "Angel hair, angel hair," she gasped. "Get it off me."

Sam figured out the way to get it off was to pinch webbing between his fingers and peel it strand by strand. "Pinch and pull," he told her. "When I pull it off, it turns into jelly and then disappears."

Dory looked like an insect trapped by a spider and wrapped in its webbing. Sam reached into Owen's pack, found his Scout knife, and began cutting Dory out of the mess. Once he'd cut the sticky strands, they turned into goo and disintegrated.

"What did you call this gunk?"

"Angel hair. It's what's left behind right after an alien visitation." Dory brushed away the last strand of webbing, watching in disgust as it dissolved. She wiped her hands on her jeans.

"Visitation? As in, they've been here in person?"

Dory snapped, "That's what I just said."

Sam ignored Dory's crankiness. His heart thudded. That's what was wrong with the plan!

"What if the professor was incorrect about these visitors being a Class One alien encounter?" Sam sounded dead worried. "What if the aliens are at the next stage, Class Two or whatever? What if they're here, up close and personal?"

"Of course they are. I just said angel hair is from..." Dory's head jerked. "Oh."

One more thing, Sam thought suddenly. "If aliens can do all that, they're smart. Who cares if the professor thinks they're not much more advanced than knuckle-dragging cavemen."

"And your point?" Dory said in a worried voice.

"My point is, wouldn't they also be smart enough to know if one of their nanochips has been deactivated?"

Somebody screamed inside Sinistrus Mansion.

Khallie!

✕ 29 ✕

THIS CAN'T BE GOOD

SAM AND DORY ran toward Sinistrus Mansion. Green mist clung to the gate's iron railings. Broken shutters banged against the shingled walls. Black windows stared at them like the eyes of a deranged witch.

The menacing, hulking shadow waited.

Sam and Dory trampled seagrass and circled the house before their steps faltered at the broken window. That odd sour smell burned the back of Sam's throat, and his heart pounded. *Get out, get out, get out,* his brain was shouting.

All he could think about was when he was five and being convinced a monster was hiding under his bed. He'd been terrified.

"Why do I keep thinking of that morning I woke up and saw a pimple on the end of my nose?" said Dory. She let out a small groan. "What a horrific moment that was."

"It's the gas. It's as if this is a special fright gas the aliens use to keep people away."

"It's working." Dory began backing away from the house.

Sam pinched his nostrils shut. "Ploog yer nowse." His heart rate began slowing.

"You sound like an idiot." But Dory did the same.

Sam peered inside the window. Inky blackness stared out.

"Hwm I sppos'ed to keep ma noose plooged and climb inside?" said Dory.

Sam opened Owen's pack, hoping to find a scarf to cover his face. Instead, stuffed neatly in a side pocket were painter masks. He pulled out two, slipped the elastic of one over his head, and breathed into the mask's gauzy shell. "Try this." He handed the other one to Dory.

Also in the pack, Owen had a tiny steel hammer, the kind people used in emergencies to punch out car windshields. Sam quickly tapped the jagged glass around the window so it was easier for him and Dory to crawl through.

Another shrill scream pierced the air.

Sam and Dory ran for the cellar stairs. Past the rickety steps leading under the foundation, they climbed down the precision-cut stone stairs. Sam hesitated on the threshold of the eerie, old-fashioned laboratory.

Dory slammed him from behind. "Could you signal when you stop?" she vented. "Yikes. That's not good."

Now it was like three hearts hammered in Sam's chest, throbbing in his throat and ears. Staring into the musty darkness past the metallic lab tables and cabinets, he saw Khallie backing up against the far wall. With one hand she held up Owen's transmitter. With her other hand, she was waving what looked like a metal table leg as she fended off four of the high schoolers in the zombie troop. An army of cats was hissing as they approached her.

What Khallie didn't see was a thin crack along the wall behind her, and from that crack bled a phosphorescent green light. Sam and Owen had missed the door earlier because it blended in with the stone. Only now it was beginning to open!

For once Sam didn't hesitate. He shot across the lab, his sneakers kicking up clouds of dust that would have sent Owen to the hospital with his asthma. He skidded through the zombie troop, colliding with Dane Parsons and sending him into a face plant.

"Sorry," said Sam. As a girl's fingers grazed his shoulder, the lights blinked out, plunging them all into darkness— except for the witch light and the tiny red light pulsating on Owen's transmitter.

"I cut the lights. That should slow the zombie kids," shouted Dory. "They still have to see, right?"

Something banged up against the *other* side of the door. The reverberations made Sam's teeth grind together.

"Khallie, shove that metal table over here!" he shouted. He could barely make out her shape in the eerie green murk. "Help me barricade the door."

"Why?" Khallie asked. "Shouldn't we wire up the receiver?"

Another crash against the door almost sent Sam spinning.

"What... was... that?" Khallie gulped.

"Let's just say the professor should have classified these aliens as a Class One *and a Half* Civilization."

The door shook with the next crash and a bigger crack of green light outlined the door. A cat bumped into Sam and scratched his ankle, causing him to let out a small yelp. Then he saw a tiny beam of light from Dory's key chain.

"Stay still, will you?" Dory told Angel Chan. She'd pulled out Owen's electromagnet from his pack and was trying to deactivate Angel's chip. But Angel wouldn't stand still, so Dory spun her around and sent her shuffling into another direction. Then she moved toward Dane Parsons.

In the murky greenlight, it looked like Dory was in a video game because of the way she kept shoving the zombie troop and wayward cats into each other and sending them in other directions.

Khallie dragged the metal table to the door and turned it on its side. Sam helped her slide it against the door. Then they shoved a metal filing cabinet against it, and added a few cat cages for extra measure. Sam pushed his shoulder against the barricade.

"Set up the receiver, Khallie."

Suddenly it was quiet behind the door. Then the lights in the lab snapped back on. Sam, Dory, and Khallie stared in amazement as the four teens lined up quickly in formation and began shuffling out of the lab and up the stairs. The cats circled once, then hunkered down and fell asleep.

"This can't be good," gulped Sam.

"Don't look a gift horse in the mouth," said Dory. "Even my friend Angel's a pain with that stupid zombie chip."

Sam didn't say that the Trojans would have been better off had they looked inside their gift horse's mouth.

The green light behind the door grew brighter. Screeching echoed through the laboratory.

"We'd better hurry!" shouted Sam.

× 30 ×

TOO TERRIFIED
TO SCREAM

DORY HUSTLED the sleeping cats into their cages and began hauling them out of the basement. "I'm getting them out of here," she called down to Sam. "Owen said when the message gets transmitted, no one should be in the basement. I assume that also means the cats."

"Good idea," grunted Sam as he shoved himself harder against the barricade.

Khallie began unravelling wires and looking for a place to hook up the receiver. "Owen said we need a metal pole."

"What about the pendant lamps?" said Sam. He pointed to the old-fashioned metallic lights dangling from the ceiling.

"Perfect." Khallie grabbed a chair and placed it on top of a long, narrow table. She climbed on top of the chair.

The door behind Sam shuddered. He pressed his back against the vibrations and held his breath, watching Khallie set up the receiver. The floor shook beneath him.

Khallie balanced on the wobbly chair, winding red and black wires around the pole of a dangling metal lamp.

Dory returned. "Weird. Those zombie kids scooped up the cat cages, and I barely escaped. Now they're moving creepily fast back to that mechanical bridge." She bent over and caught her breath. "What are you doing?"

"Saving the world, I hope," Sam grunted as he pinned himself harder against the barricade.

"Could you reach into my messenger bag and pass me Owen's pliers?" asked Khallie. "Um, quickly?"

Dory handed Khallie red-handled pliers.

"Do you think the zombie brigade got a signal to clear out?" Sam asked. His heart started hammering. *Hurry*, he thought but didn't say.

Khallie snipped wires and then held the pliers in her teeth while she stretched and wound the black wire to the receiver. When she was done, she took the pliers out of her mouth. "I hope the receiver can hang from the ceiling like this. Did Owen say it would work if I left it hanging in the air?"

A deep thrumming began. The door behind Sam shook harder. "Are there any loose connections?"

Khallie tightened a screw. "No."

BANG! SLAM!

"Turn the switch on!" Sam shouted. Dory threw herself against the barricade beside Sam as the door made a strange buckling motion, almost like an ocean wave.

The receiver's red light blinked on. It pulsated three times...

Then the light turned green. Message sent.

The door exploded open, sending Dory and Sam up in the air and then down on their hands and knees a metre away.

The chair Khallie had been standing on toppled, and the table tipped over. Khallie held onto the pendant lamp, her legs bicycling in the air. A scream rose in Sam's mouth like a bubble waiting to burst and then stuck there. He hadn't known a person could be too terrified to scream.

From behind the gaping door, blinding green light poured out from the tunnel. Standing just inside were three silhouettes looking like something Sam had once seen in a carnival funhouse mirror.

It was as if Sam was watching a film in slow motion—it took so long for his brain to accept what his eyes were seeing...

The shadows were tall, really tall, with long, really long, thin legs and arms. Their silhouetted heads seemed too large, perched on necks that were too long. Their heads moved on those necks like bobble-head dolls. No, not quite, they swerved and swivelled like the ends of insect antennae.

"I'm going to puke." Dory started retching.

Hanging from the lamp, Khallie spun her legs even faster, as if she was trying to run away.

Suddenly a high-pitched screech sounded from the depths of the tunnel, and the shadows disappeared.

Sam ran and grabbed Khallie's legs, and together they tumbled to the ground. They jumped up and tore out of the basement. Dory scooped up Owen's pack and took the steps two at a time. As they all raced out of Sinistrus Mansion, explosions rumbled beneath their feet.

Sam got ready to flee, but then he checked over his shoulder and saw Dory just standing there. "What?" he snapped.

"I..." she shook her head. "I just need a minute."

"We might not have a minute," said Khallie. Sam couldn't argue with that.

"I... want to make sure Angel and the others are okay." Dory dodged behind the trees.

Sam drew a ragged breath. In his terror he'd panicked and forgotten all about the zombie kids. Khallie ran after Dory, and Sam followed on her heels.

They reached the end of the grounds and stumbled through the thicket. Then Sam almost slammed into Khallie. He looked over her and Dory's shoulders.

"I don't believe it," Dory said. "It's like the thing is alive."

The mechanical bridge was moving, first like a wriggling snake forcing the last zombie kid, Angel, to jump. She waded waist-deep in the surf and held a cat cage over her head as she made it back to shore. Then the articulated metallic arm of the bridge writhed and rose out of the water, snapping and lashing.

"Like the tentacle of a giant squid," Khallie said breathlessly.

The arm flipped backwards and crashed against the shore, shaking leaves off the arbutus tree they were under. Another gigantic splash and the arm dived under water in a boiling froth of foam.

"Run!" shouted Sam. They tore across the island as the ground beneath their feet buckled. Jumping over scrub, slashing their way through seagrass, tripping on rocks, they half-slid down the bluff. Dory stood up on shaky legs and gasped, "This pack weighs a ton."

"Leave it," said Sam.

"No way," said Dory. She swallowed and caught her breath. "Your friend's got enough parts in here for any emergency." Huffing and puffing, she broke into another run. They scrambled across the rocks and ran onto the wharf.

Waves smashed against the rocks. The dilapidated dock moaned against the crashing surf. From out of nowhere a horrible storm had set in. Thunder boomed, lightning shot across the night sky, and green clouds rose from Sinistrus Mansion. Sam thought they looked like plumes of smoke from a witch's giant cauldron.

"Get on the boat!" shouted Blake. "We thought you were goners."

Peaceful Dream bobbed like a bathtub toy as the waves grew large and menacing. The surface of the island trembled, and more rocks began sliding and rolling into the water. Sam undid the casting line and held it taut as Khallie and Dory leaped from the swaying dock onto the boat.

Sam reached for the edge of the sailboat, only for the wharf to sway to the other side. Then he did a running leap and jumped, but missed, grabbing the rail. He started sliding.

An arm shot out and grabbed him by the elbow, and Khallie hauled him on board. "Told you I'll do the rescuing," she smiled.

"I recall fending off a few zombies and aliens for you," Sam shot back.

"You're right. We have each other's backs." Khallie nodded.

"Hey, Owen, if ever there's an apocalypse, I want to be on your team," said Dory. She handed him back his pack. Owen grinned as he pulled on the throttle. But the engine didn't turn.

"I knew we'd used too much gas." Blake shook his head. "No worries. Hoist the main sail."

"How?" asked Sam.

"Pull that mast thing toward you, no, um, that one. I think. Ah, yank off those blue cloth ties and unfurl the main sail."

Peaceful Dream crept away from the dock as Blake steered the rudder with the tiller, and Owen, Sam, and Khallie operated the main sail. Dory hung over the edge of the boat. Sam heard more retching. Dory sat up suddenly and pointed to the choppy waves.

"What's that?"

Orange and yellow balls of light pulsated below the surface of the water, getting rounder and brighter until the ocean radiated with an eerie glow. From below the surface, a deep rumbling sounded as though the sea bed was splitting apart.

"Now that's a *slowdown* echo!" cried Blake over the thundering roar. The water around them whipped and boiled, splashing onto the deck as huge, frothy waves bounced the sailboat around.

Peaceful Dream tossed and rolled as it circled toward a giant whirlpool.

× 31 ×

A TERRIBLE NIGHTMARE

SAM TRIED HANGING onto the deck railing as the sailboat tipped up and down, and then swayed starboard and port. They were being tossed back and forth across the deck like Ping-Pong balls.

"We've got to pull out of this." Blake used both hands to yank the tiller, directing their sailboat away from the whirlpool. For every metre he gained, they lost two as the whirlpool grew larger.

"Angle the jib sail parallel to the main sail!" Owen shouted over the roar. "That will give us more speed."

"Huh?" shouted Sam. Owen did a lot of pointing.

Waves crashed against their sailboat's hull. The jib sail flapped above Sam's head as he pulled the rope.

"Secure that rope on the clam cleat beside you," shouted Owen.

The rope left burns along Sam's palms. *Peaceful Dream* tipped menacingly on its side as Khallie, Dory, and Owen hung on. Salt spray coated Sam's face.

"*Peaceful Dream*," groaned Dory. "This boat should be called *Terrible Nightmare*." Her face was as green as the fog that surrounded them.

A huge clap of thunder exploded over their heads and wind whipped around, slashing the sails.

"Prepare to jib!" shouted Owen.

"Huh?" asked Khallie.

"Watch out for the boom!" Blake shouted, and Sam and Khallie ducked just in time as the horizontal beam extending from the mast swung across the deck.

"Tack!" shouted Blake.

Sam reached for the rope Owen was pointing to and pulled it tight.

"Jib again," Blake ordered.

Sam leaped to the other side of the sailboat and grabbed the rope for the jib sail. Back and forth, back and forth, Owen and Sam tacked and jibbed. Khallie held the winch, and whenever the sail rope was too hard to pull, she'd stick the winch in the clam cleat and torque the rope.

Peaceful Dream tipped port side, then back to starboard.

"I bet we're travelling eight knots," Owen said, sounding impressed.

"How fast is that in regular speed?" asked Kallie.

"Too fast," groaned Dory, clutching her stomach.

Sam pulled the rope. "Winch," he called, and Khallie handed him the metal lever that fit inside the cleat. Then he torqued it. He torqued hard.

They pulled out of the whirlpool's deathly trap.

"We're tilting too close to the water," shouted Owen. Waves crested the boat rails and water splashed on deck. "Blake, take your hands off the tiller and the boat will sail into the wind, righting itself!"

"Oh, yeah," said Blake. He eased up on the tiller. The boat bobbed upright. "Good call."

There was the sound of a huge fan blasting, and the air around them swirled and shredded the green fog.

"Look!" Owen shouted.

Barely visible in the swirling green light, Sam spotted two gigantic, triangular objects breaking out of the water and rising. The fog formed into two treacherous funnel clouds looming above. The shadows hovered for only a split second, shot straight up, and then disappeared.

For several minutes everyone stayed silent as they sailed around the corner of the island and toward the mainland.

"Did we just kick alien butt?" Blake held fast to the tiller.

Sam was glad he wasn't too terrified to laugh.

⨉ 32 ⨉

WE COULD HAVE
A BLAST

THEY CROSSED the breakwater and sailed smoothly to the shore and back to the yacht club wharf. Sam thought they *almost* docked the boat perfectly. There was only a minor collision and a small scratch on *Peaceful Dream*'s hull.

"My dad's gonna kill me," said Blake.

"Yeah, well, I'm sure that's overdue," Khallie smirked. "You've been getting away with murder for way too long."

"Maybe," Blake said.

Sam and Khallie leaped off *Peaceful Dream,* and as Sam tied the rope to the wharf, Khallie pulled the wheelchair down the ramp until she was beside the boat.

Uneasiness crossed Khallie's face. "Do you need me to...?"

Blake shook his head fiercely, but then his face softened. "No, I think I'll be fine with help from my new sailing crew," he said, nodding at Sam and Owen.

"Seriously?" Owen's eyes widened.

"Want to join the sailing team with me?" asked Blake. "The three of us could smoke the competition."

"I'm in," Sam said enthusiastically. How could he be afraid of a sailing competition? He'd just beaten back an alien invasion.

"Ahem," said Khallie.

"I mean, the four of us," Blake corrected himself. Then he looked Dory's way. "Or..."

"Don't even say it." Dory still looked green—and it wasn't any reflection from the fog. "I'm not crossing water deeper than my ankles for a very long time."

While Dory drove Khallie and Owen home, Sam pushed Blake's wheelchair along the ramp and back to Blake's street. Going up was definitely not as fun as coming down.

The black and still night made it seem as if the last hours had never happened. Even the fog had lifted. Clouds scudded across the sky, revealing a gold harvest moon sinking into the horizon and a scattering of stars around Orion's Belt.

Except... stargazing would never be the same again.

As they rounded the corner behind Blake's house, Sam detected shaking leaves in the hedge beside Blake's property. Someone was behind the bush. Blake stopped, and Sam parted the branches.

"Hello, Professor," Sam said.

Professor Marigold turned around and stepped away from the bluff. He'd been yanking his hydrophone out of the ocean, and it dangled in his hand, covered in briny-smelling kelp and dripping salt water onto the ground.

"Hello, boys," he said pleasantly, as if it *wasn't* the middle of the night, and as if they *hadn't* just fought back an alien invasion.

"So I guess you know, Professor," Sam said awkwardly. "The plan worked."

"Well done," Professor Marigold said. "Have a nice evening." He packed the hydrophone into his black leather satchel.

That was it? That's all he had to say?

Blake shot forward in his wheelchair.

"Professor Marigold, I was, ah, wondering…"

"Yes?" The little man adjusted his glasses and stared intently. He was eye-level with Blake.

"You seem to know a lot about advanced technology, and I was wondering if you could make a diagram or write some instructions that would make me as good as new." Blake's face was guarded.

"You seem quite good already and reasonably *new* in human years. Do you mean new as in using your legs?" asked the professor.

"Yes, so I can run and ski and do high jumps again," explained Blake.

Professor Marigold sighed softly. "Son, this planet is young, and your Class Three-Quarters Civilization is still violent. I'm afraid people have a way to go before certain technology wouldn't be misused."

Blake waited.

"If a diagram of the *wrong* technology fell into the *wrong* hands," the professor explained, "it would be like giving a five-year-old a button that would detonate an atomic bomb... only worse."

Sam thought of Molly. Sweet little Molly—yeah, that would be a total disaster!

"I... understand," Blake said quietly. He turned his wheelchair.

"Wait," said the professor. "People here are very smart. Even children on this planet can outwit a Class One Civilization."

"I'd say those aliens were a Class One and a Half, sir," corrected Sam.

"Interesting," said the professor. He adjusted his lab coat. In a softer tone he said, "Well, the Class Three-Quarters Civilization that we have here is on the verge of amazing discoveries. Yes, just around the corner there will be big medical advances. And I expect with hard work and time and physiotherapy, you'll make progress, Blake."

The professor turned and scurried away, his black leather satchel flapping behind him.

Blake called after him, "That's good to hear." Then he muttered, "Even if it's no different than what my doctors told me."

Blake looked at Sam. "I was hoping I could be like a regular person even sooner."

Sam didn't know what to say, but the soft voice inside him whispered, *Sammy, don't just stand there. You have to say something.*

"Is anyone really a regular person?" Sam shrugged.

Blake cocked his head. "Yeah, I get it, but I love sports."

"Like rowing in dangerous currents," agreed Sam.

"And sailing." Blake's face lit up.

"Don't forget bobsledding," Sam grinned. "Only snow would work better than sand."

"That's true." Blake smiled. "We could have a blast."

A light turned on in the upstairs window of Blake's house. "I'd better go." He rolled his chair to the elevator his parents had set up at the back of the house. "See you soon, Sam."

"Psst, Sam, do you think you might want to hustle a little?" Dory had left her car parked down the street. "If Babcia discovers we're out, we're toast. Remember, Dad's coming home soon."

Sam had forgotten all about that. He'd felt such relief at solving the mystery of Croaker Island's phantom echoes, he'd forgotten about his other problems.

Sam and Dory drove home in complete silence.

× 33 ×

A BEAUTIFUL
FRIENDSHIP

"SAM, SAMMY, SAM-SAM, wake up!"

Sam groaned. He opened his bleary eyes and gazed at his little sister staring at him, nose to nose. Something furry batted his cheek. Pix.

"What?" He tried to turn over, which didn't work so well with Pix on his stomach.

"A big surprise, Sammy, c'mon," Molly tugged at his quilt.

Sam sat up. "What surprise?"

"I'm not allowed to say." Molly's chin dimpled even when she frowned. "But I will give you one hint. It's someone we've been missing a lot."

"Dad?"

"Was that too big of a hint?" Molly's brow creased with worry. "I'm not supposed to ruin the surprise."

Sam shot out of bed and shooed Molly and Pix out of his room. He yanked on his jeans and T-shirt, and then tugged his least brightly coloured sweater over his head.

The kitchen was deserted, the dishes had even been washed, and the clock said 10:30. He could smell leaves burning out back. Sam rushed into the yard.

Babcia, Dory, and Molly stood on the grass under the steely grey sky. Babcia appeared... wary, and so did Dory. Only Molly beamed.

Captain Jake Novak had heaped piles of leaves and branches and lit a big bonfire. The sharp tang of leaf-smoke billowed. His father had just arrived and had already cleaned up the backyard!

"You've been AWOL, soldier," said his father. "Sleeping your life away while we've been waiting for you. Grab some more branches and help me with this fire."

"Yes, sir." Sam got to it.

Once all the branches had been dumped into the fire, Captain Jake took off his work gloves, wiped soot off his face with his shirt sleeve, and held out his hand. "Come on."

Sam went to shake his dad's hand, but his father wrapped him in a hug that rivalled Molly's. He'd forgotten how comforting that could feel. But still... Why was his father here?

As if reading his mind, Captain Jake said, "Line up, troop. I have an announcement to make."

Sam joined Dory and Molly. Molly slipped her hand into Sam's. It trembled slightly.

"We're going to move into a bigger house in the Cove," said the captain.

"So, we're staying?" Sam shouted. "Like, forever?" His heart soared.

"Not just us," their father said cryptically.

"Um, pardon?" asked Dory.

Captain Jake Novak drew himself arrow-straight. He smiled and his eyes wrinkled. "I have an announcement to make. I'm bringing someone here over the holidays for you to meet—someone who I really want you to make welcome."

"What kind of someone?" Dory asked suspiciously.

"My soon-to-be wife," said the captain.

Sam felt sucker-punched. He drew in a sharp breath.

"A new mom?" Molly asked hopefully.

"Not just a mom, but two new sisters," the captain laughed, "at least for the holidays. I'll be introducing you to Lieutenant Sally soon-to-be Novak, and her twin daughters, Alice and Abby."

"And they're all staying with us?" Sam gasped.

Sam thought he heard Babcia mutter.

"Sometimes," said Captain Novak.

Four sisters? Sam would be tripping over fuzzy slippers and cutie-pie stuffed animals, and the house would always stink of perfume. This was terrible news! What was it

Babcia always said? "Be careful what you wish for." He'd wished for a permanent home, but he'd rather face another alien invasion then live with a flock of girls.

Dory took Molly's hand when Molly reached out. "Will I still be your bestest sister?" Molly whispered, tightening her hold on Sam's and Dory's hands.

"Always," they said at once.

"I bet I surprised you with that news," said their father.

"Yes, Daddy."

"Uh-huh."

"I guess."

"Hmm."

When they went inside the cottage, Babcia heated up hot chocolate and helped Sam make cinnamon toast. They sat around the breakfast table catching up. Dory's cellphone buzzed. She started texting, ignoring her father's frown.

"Sam, George from *Unexplained Phenomena* texted me." Dory sounded excited. "He's convinced the Coast Guard to check out Croaker's Island. They're on the island now."

"Can we go see the Coast Guard?" Sam asked Babcia. His grandmother raised her eyebrows and pointed to the captain. "Oops, I mean, Dad, can we go?"

"I just got here."

"I won't leave you," said Molly, tangling their father in one of her boa constrictor hugs. "Can you take me to the fall fair? There's a parrot ride I love."

"Looks like I have plans, anyway," their dad said to them. Sam and Dory raced for her car. "I'm glad to see you two are getting along so well," their father called after them. "And, Sam, it's good to hear you're joining the rowing team."

"Uh-huh," Sam called back.

"Don't track your muddy sneakers on my new car mat," Dory grumbled.

Sam tried to keep his feet in the air as he used Dory's phone to call Khallie, Blake, and Owen.

$$\times \quad \times \quad \times$$

IT SEEMED AS IF half the town had lined the shore across from Croaker's Island after the Coast Guard docked. Sam figured the *Unexplained Phenomena* podcast was more popular than he'd guessed possible. Or maybe that wasn't so strange. Others must have noticed some of the peculiar goings-on in this town.

Two men in uniform disembarked from the ship and began gesturing wildly at George the podcast guy.

"OMG, there's Blake's brother," Dory gushed. They walked toward Colton, Blake, and Khallie. Dory waved madly. Blake and Khallie waved back, and then Colton waved.

"OMG. Did he just wave at me?" Dory almost freaked. Then in a darker voice, she said, "Sam. Who is that?" She stopped in her tracks and narrowed her eyes.

Colton had turned away and become very engaged in conversation with the dark-haired Azina. "That's Khallie's sister."

Sam could tell by all the laughing that they were hitting it off super well.

"Hi, Sam."

Owen raced toward them. "Did you hear? They found nothing on the island. Well, not nothing. They found all the missing cats. But get this: there is *no laboratory*, only what they thought might be a rock slide in one of the caves under the island. No evidence of any kind of aliens or anything. They're yelling at that podcast guy and calling him a menace and..."

Sam was hardly listening. He was staring over at Khallie and Blake. She'd obviously introduced him to her sister, and now she was talking earnestly to him. Her face looked so serious. When she finished, Blake reached over and hugged her.

Sam was happy for Khallie and Blake. So why did it feel like someone had just shoved a dagger in his heart?

"Mercury is in retrograde," Dory said miserably. "It looks like you and I, Sam, are unlucky in love."

"It's cool," said Sam. He had them both as friends, and he had Owen. He was staying in Croaker's Cove. It was everything he'd wished for… sort of…

"We'd better stick together," said Dory. "I mean, we fended off aliens, so we can sort Dad out about his crazy idea of marrying for a third time, especially to a woman with twins."

Sam was on board with that. He quoted a line from an old movie he'd seen once: "You know, Dory, this could be the beginning of a beautiful friendship."

"Don't get carried away," Dory snapped.

THE END

×

ACKNOWLEDGEMENTS

WITH APPRECIATION to the Heritage House team: Lara Kordic, who liked *Croaker's Island* from the beginning; Lesley Cameron, for her editorial direction; and Leslie Kenny, who runs the marketing. Your support is appreciated. Thank you also to a couple of great writers of adventure and fun for younger readers: Ari Goelman (I started the story sooner) and Sean Klein (I paid more attention to detail). Both of you gave such valuable feedback! Much thanks to Doug Hill for his sailing tips, and it goes without saying that any errors are mine and not his. Also thank you to John for caring about my writing as much if not more than me, and to Alec and Joey for their continued interest.

×

ABOUT
THE AUTHOR

LINDA DEMEULEMEESTER lives on the west coast and thinks the ocean is very mysterious indeed...

She has worked in the fields of literacy and education as a teacher and a program advisor, and is the author of the popular and critically acclaimed Grim Hill series. The first book in the series, *The Secret of Grim Hill,* won the prestigious Silver Birch Award and was named one of Canadian Toy Testing Council's Best Books. Other books in the spooky tween series have been nominated and shortlisted for several awards.

Discover Linda DeMeulemeester's Grim Hill Series, available from Heritage House/Wandering Fox and wherever fine books are sold!

- *The Secret of Grim Hill*
- *The Secret Deepens*
- *The Forgotten Secret*
- *The Family Secret*
- *Forest of Secrets*
- *Carnival of Secrets*